Matt glanced at h ***followed her into the hall,*** ***knew he was eager to head back over to the park.***

But when they made their way down the stairs and into the empty living room, he frowned.

"Where did the babysitter go?"

"I sent her home." She hoped she sounded more confident than she felt, because now that they were really alone, her stomach was in such a mess of knots she didn't think they'd ever untangle.

"I thought we were going back to the park to see the fireworks."

"I changed my mind."

"Don't I get a vote?"

She shook her head. "No, but you have a choice."

"What choice is that?" Matt asked her.

She lifted her arms to link them around his neck. "You can go back to the park for the fireworks—" her fingers cupped the back of his head, drew it down toward hers "—or we can make some of our own right here."

And then she kissed him.

Dear Reader,

Having grown up with each of a sister and a brother, I understand the importance and endurance of the sibling bond. So when I created the Garrett brothers—Matthew, Jackson and Lukas—I knew they would share a close connection. No doubt they would have different ideas and opinions (and moments of disagreement), but when it really mattered, they would stand by one another.

As Matt starts to fall for the young widow next door (and her adorable children), his brothers can't help but be concerned. Georgia Reed assures them she doesn't have time for romance—with four-year-old twins and a four-month-old baby, she barely has time to do the laundry! But she finds it increasingly difficult to resist her engaging neighbor....

So when Matt proposes, what can Jack and Luke do except offer to stand up for him at the wedding? Because brothers support one another through difficult times and celebrate together when life is good.

Of course, they might debate whether marriage is a cause for commiseration or jubilation, but that's another story. Actually two more stories. In the meantime, I hope you enjoy Matt and Georgia's.

Happy reading,

Brenda Harlen

FROM NEIGHBORS... TO NEWLYWEDS?

BRENDA HARLEN

ISBN-13: 978-0-373-65717-9

FROM NEIGHBORS...TO NEWLYWEDS?

This edition published by arrangement with Harlequin Books S.A.

For questions and comments about the quality of this book, please contact us at CustomerService@Harlequin.com.

www.Harlequin.com

Printed in U.S.A.

Books by Brenda Harlen

Harlequin Special Edition

***Prince Daddy & the Nanny* #2147
***Royal Holiday Bride* #2160
‡‡*The Maverick's Ready-Made Family* #2215
¤¤*From Neighbors... to Newlyweds?* #2235

Silhouette Special Edition

**Her Best-Kept Secret* #1756
The Marriage Solution #1811
†*One Man's Family* #1827
The New Girl in Town #1859
***The Prince's Royal Dilemma* #1898
***The Prince's Cowgirl Bride* #1920
††*Family in Progress* #1928
***The Prince's Holiday Baby* #1942
§*The Texas Tycoon's Christmas Baby* #2016
¤*The Engagement Project* #2021
¤*The Pregnancy Plan* #2038
¤*The Baby Surprise* #2056
‡*Thunder Canyon Homecoming* #2079
***The Prince's Second Chance* #2100

Harlequin Romantic Suspense

McIver's Mission #1224
Some Kind of Hero #1246
Extreme Measures #1282
Bulletproof Hearts #1313
Dangerous Passions #1394

*Family Business
†Logan's Legacy Revisited
**Reigning Men
††Back in Business
§The Foleys and the McCords
¤Brides & Babies
‡Montana Mavericks: Thunder Canyon Cowboys
‡‡Montana Mavericks: Back in the Saddle
¤¤Those Engaging Garretts!

Other books by Brenda Harlen available in ebook format.

BRENDA HARLEN

grew up in a small town, surrounded by books and imaginary friends. Although she always dreamed of being a writer, she chose to follow a more traditional career path first. After two years of practicing as an attorney (including an appearance in front of the Supreme Court of Canada), she gave up her "real" job to be a mom and to try her hand at writing books. Three years, five manuscripts and another baby later, she sold her first book—an RWA Golden Heart winner—to Silhouette Books.

Brenda lives in southern Ontario with her real-life husband/hero, two heroes-in-training and two neurotic dogs. She is still surrounded by books (too many books, according to her children) and imaginary friends, but she also enjoys communicating with real people. Readers can contact Brenda by email at brendaharlen@yahoo.com or by snail mail c/o Harlequin Books, 233 Broadway, Suite 1001, New York, NY 10279.

Because this series is about brothers,
this book is dedicated to Brett (AKA "BIL").

You became my brother when you married my sister, and through all the years that you've been part of our family you've proven yourself to be a terrific husband and a wonderful father—a true romantic hero.

(P.S. You're a pretty good brother-in-law, too.)

Chapter One

The house was finally, blissfully quiet.

Georgia Reed mentally crossed her fingers as she sat down at the antique dining room table, hoping for one hour. If she could have a full sixty minutes to focus on the manuscript pages spread out in front of her, she might actually catch up on her work. Unfortunately, the thought of catching a nap was much more tempting than the book she was currently reading.

Though she was officially on maternity leave from her job as an associate editor at Tandem Publishing, she had agreed to accept work on a contract basis to help out the senior editor and keep some money coming in. It had seemed like a good idea at the time, but Georgia hadn't been nearly as productive as she'd hoped to be, especially since she'd uprooted her kids and moved to Pinehurst only six weeks earlier.

She sipped from the cup of herbal tea she'd reheated for a third time and skimmed through the previous chapter to refresh her memory. But just as her mind began to focus on the story, it occurred to her that it was *too* quiet.

The realization kicked her protective instincts into overdrive. She pushed her chair away from the table and raced across the hall to the living room, where she'd left four-year-old Quinn and Shane with a pile of building blocks. The carpet was littered with the chunky pieces but her boys were both gone—no doubt through the wide-open patio door.

The door had been closed when she settled the boys down to play—closed *and* locked. But the lock was tricky, and sometimes just tugging on the handle would allow the latch to slip and the lock to slide free. She'd talked to her mother about getting it fixed, but apparently that detail had slipped Charlotte's mind.

And now her children were gone.

She hurried back to the dining room to grab the baby monitor before racing out the back door.

"Quinn! Shane!" She ran across the deck, cursing when she stepped on a red block. They couldn't have gone far. She'd only left them in the room a few minutes earlier. If anything had happened—

No, she couldn't even complete the thought.

"Quinn! Shane!"

A flash of movement caught the corner of her eye, and she spun around, her heart sinking when she didn't see the boys' familiar faces but the shadowed jaw of a grown man standing on the grass.

"Are you looking for two little guys about yay—" he held a hand about three and a half feet off the ground "—high?"

"Did you see where they went?" she asked hopefully, desperately.

"They wandered into my backyard." He gestured toward the adjoining property.

Georgia closed her eyes so he wouldn't see that they'd filled with tears. "Oh, thank you, God."

"Actually, my name's Matt—Matt Garrett."

She opened her eyes again and saw that he was smiling at her.

"And your kids are fine," he promised her.

"Only until I get my hands on them," she muttered.

His smile widened.

Now that the panic had subsided and her heart was beating more normally again, she took a moment to look at her new neighbor—and felt a little tug low in her belly.

Matt Garrett had thick dark hair that was sexily tousled, as if he'd been running his fingers through it, a slightly crooked nose and a strong unshaven jaw. His shoulders were broad, his long, lean body well-muscled. And as his deep blue gaze connected with her own, she felt a subtle buzz in her veins that made her feel hot and tingly in a way that she hadn't experienced in a very long time.

"One of the puppies escaped into your yard and caught their attention," he explained.

"Puppies?"

"Come and check them out," he invited.

She hooked the monitor on her belt and followed him, surreptitiously checking out his spectacular backside as she did so.

He'd moved in a few days earlier. She'd noticed the moving truck when she'd gone out to the porch to check the mail Wednesday afternoon—and then she'd noticed the tall, broad-shouldered man supervising the unloading of it.

He was in faded denim with an even more faded Orioles T-shirt stretched across his broad chest. Definitely a man's man, she decided, and felt a flutter of something low in her belly. He lifted an arm in casual greeting and flashed a quick smile that actually made Georgia's heart skip a beat before it began hammering against her ribs.

She raised her hand in response, waving her mail at him, then felt the flood of heat in her cheeks as she realized what she'd done. She wasn't sure if it was sexual deprivation or sleep deprivation that was responsible for her distraction, but thankfully, he was too far away to note either her instinctive physical response or her embarrassment. But wow—the man obviously had some potent sex appeal if he could affect her from such a distance.

An appeal that, she knew now, was further magnified up close.

"This is Luke—and Jack," Matt told her, gesturing to the two other men on his porch in turn. "My brothers."

The former was even taller than her six-foot-tall neighbor, with the same brown hair but blue-green eyes; the latter was of similar height but with broader shoulders and slightly darker hair. All three were sinfully handsome.

"I'm Georgia," she finally said, her heart rate mostly back to normal now that the twins were in her line of sight again. "And these pint-sized Houdinis are Quinn and Shane."

"What's a Houdini?" Quinn tore his attention away from the blanket-lined laundry basket for the first time since she'd stepped onto her neighbor's porch.

"A little boy who is in very serious trouble for leaving the house without his mommy," she admonished.

Her son's gaze dropped to his feet, a telltale sign of guilt. "We just wanted to see the puppies."

"Puppies," Shane echoed, and looked up at her with the heartbreakingly sweet smile that never failed to remind her of his father.

She took a few steps closer, as inexorably drawn to the basket as her children had been. But still, she had to make sure they understood that leaving the house for any reason wasn't acceptable.

"If you wanted to see the puppies, you should have told Mommy that you wanted to see the puppies," she said.

"But you told us not to bug you 'cuz you had work to do," Quinn reminded her.

And it was exactly what she'd said when she set them up with their blocks.

"I also told you to never go anywhere—even outside into the backyard—without telling me first."

But how could she blame them for being drawn away when even her heart had sighed at the first glimpse of those white, brown and black bodies wriggling around in the basket?

She looked at her neighbor again. "You have *four* puppies?"

"No." Matt shook his head emphatically. "*I* don't have *any* puppies—they're all Luke's."

"Only until I can find good homes for them," his brother said.

"How did you end up with them?" she wondered.

"I'm a vet," he told her. "And when someone finds an abandoned animal on the side of the road, it usually ends up at my clinic. In this case, the abandoned animal was a very pregnant beagle that, two days later, gave birth to eight puppies."

"Eight?" She cringed at the thought. As if carrying and birthing twins hadn't been difficult enough.

"My receptionist is taking care of the other four."

"They look kind of young to be away from their mother," she noted.

"They are," he agreed.

It was all he said, but it was enough for her to understand that the mother hadn't survived the delivery—and to be grateful that his response in front of the twins wasn't any more explicit than that.

"Nice puppy," Shane said, gently patting the top of a tiny head.

"Can we keep one?" Quinn, always the more talkative and articulate twin, asked her.

She shook her head. As much as she hated to refuse her kids anything, she'd learned that there were times she had to say no. This was definitely one of those times. "I'm sorry, boys. A puppy is too much responsibility for us to take on right now."

But she didn't object when Matt lifted one of them out of the box and handed it to her. And she couldn't resist bringing it closer to nuzzle the soft, warm body. And when the little pink tongue swiped her chin, her heart absolutely melted.

"He likes you, Mom," Quinn told her.

"She," Matt corrected. "That one's a girl."

Her son wrinkled his nose. "We don't want a girl puppy."

"We don't want *any* puppy," Georgia said again, trying to sound firm.

"We *do* want a puppy," Shane insisted.

"'Cept Dr. Luke says they can't go anywhere for two more weeks," Quinn informed her. "'Cuz they're too little to eat and hafta be fed by a bottle."

Shane pouted for another minute, but the mention of eating prompted him to announce, "I'm hungry."

"So why don't we go home and I'll make some little pizzas for lunch?" she suggested.

"With pepperonis?"

"With lots of pepperoni," she promised.

But Quinn shook his head. "We don't wanna go home. We wanna stay with the daddies."

Georgia felt her cheeks burning as her gaze shifted from one man to the next.

Matt's smile slipped, just a little; Luke kept his attention firmly focused on the animals; and Jack actually took a step backward.

"They're at that age," she felt compelled to explain, "where they think every adult male is a daddy. Especially since they lost their own father."

"He's not lost, he's dead," Quinn said matter-of-factly.

The announcement made Shane's eyes fill with tears and his lower lip quiver. "I miss Daddy."

Georgia slipped her arm around his shoulders.

Matt's brows lifted. "You're a widow?"

She nodded, because her throat had tightened and she wanted to ensure she was in control of her emotions before she spoke. "My husband passed away eleven months ago." And although she'd accepted that Phillip was gone, she still missed him, and there were times—too many times—when she felt completely overwhelmed by the responsibilities of being a single parent. "That's one of the reasons I moved in here with my mom."

"Charlotte's your mother?"

"You know her?"

"I met her the first time I came to look at the house," he said. "But I haven't seen her since I moved in."

"She's on her annual trip to Vegas with some friends," Georgia told him.

"Leaving you on your own with two young boys," he remarked sympathetically.

"And a baby," she said, just as a soft coo sounded through the baby monitor she'd clipped on her belt.

"Pippa's waking up." Quinn jumped up, his desire to stay with the "daddies" not nearly as strong as his affection for his baby sister.

"Pippa," Shane echoed.

Matt looked at Georgia, seeking clarification. "You have three kids?"

She nodded. "Four-year-old twins and a four-month-old daughter."

Well, that explained the shadows under her gorgeous eyes, Matt decided. A pair of active preschoolers and a baby would wear any young mother out—especially one without a husband to help ease the burden. But even exhausted, she was one of the most beautiful women he'd ever met.

She had a heart-shaped face with creamy skin, elegantly shaped lips, a delicate nose dusted with freckles, and the bluest eyes he'd ever seen. He'd caught his first glimpse of her on moving day. She'd been casually dressed in a sleeveless yellow blouse and a pair of faded denim jeans with her honey-blond hair in a ponytail, but even from a distance, he'd felt the tug of attraction.

Standing within two feet of her now, that tug was even stronger—much stronger than any self-preservation instincts that warned him against getting involved with a woman with three children who could take hold of his heart.

"You do have your hands full," he said.

"Every day is a challenge," she agreed. And then, to the boys, "Come on—we've got to go get your sister."

"Can we bring Pippa back to see the puppies?" Quinn asked hopefully.

His mother shook her head. "In fact, you're going to apologize to Mr. Garrett for intruding—"

"Matt," he interjected, because it was friendlier than "Mister" and less daunting than "Doctor," and because he definitely wanted to be on a first-name basis with his lovely neighbor. "And it wasn't at all an intrusion. In fact, it was a pleasure to meet all of you."

"Does that mean we can come back again?" Quinn asked.

"Anytime," he said.

"And within two weeks, you'll be calling someone to put up a fence between our properties," Georgia warned.

He shook his head. "If I did that, they wouldn't be able to come over to play in the tree house."

"Mommy says we can't go in the tree house," Quinn admitted. "'Cuz it's not ours."

"But a tree house is made for little boys, and since I don't have a little boy of my own—" Matt ignored the pang of loss and longing in his heart, deliberately keeping his tone light "—it's going to need someone to visit it every once in a while, so it doesn't get lonely."

"We could visit," Quinn immediately piped up, as Shane nodded his head with enthusiasm and Georgia rolled her eyes.

"That's a great idea—so long as you check to make sure it's okay with your mom first," Matt told them.

"Can we, Mommy?"

"Pleeeease?"

He held his breath, almost as anxious for her response as the twins were. It shouldn't matter. He didn't even know this woman—but he knew that he wanted to know her, and he knew that it wouldn't be a hardship to hang out with her kids, either.

"We'll talk about it another time," she said.

Quinn let out an exaggerated sigh. "That's what she says when she means no."

"It means 'we'll talk about it another time,'" Georgia reiterated firmly.

"I'm hungry," Shane said again.

She tousled his hair. "Then we should go home to make those pizzas."

"I'm *not* hungry," Quinn said. "I wanna stay here."

"If you're not hungry, then Shane will get all the little pizzas."

Georgia's casual response earned a scowl from her son.

"And you can help us paint the deck," Matt told Quinn.

The furrow in his brow deepened. "I guess I could eat some pizza."

"I'd take the pizza over painting, too," Luke told him.

"Unfortunately, we weren't given that choice," Jack said in a conspiratorial whisper.

"And since you weren't," Matt noted, "you can go get the painting supplies."

Jack headed into the house while Luke picked up the basket full of puppies and moved it under the shade of a nearby tree so the curious canines couldn't get in the way of their work.

Shane and Quinn stayed by Georgia's side, but their eyes—

filled with an almost desperate yearning—tracked the path of the puppies. And as he looked at the twins' mother, Matt thought he understood just a little bit of what they were feeling.

In the more than three years that had passed since his divorce, Matt had wondered if he would ever feel anything more than a basic stirring of attraction for another woman. Ten minutes after meeting Georgia Reed, he could answer that question with a definitive yes.

"Thank you," she said to him now.

"For what?"

"Being so patient and tolerant with the boys."

"I like kids," he said easily.

"Then you'll like this neighborhood," she told him.

He held her gaze as his lips curved. "I already do."

Matt watched as Georgia walked away, with one of the boys' hands clasped firmly in each of hers. Obviously she wasn't willing to take any chances that they might disappear again—even on the short trek next door.

The first time he'd seen her, it hadn't occurred to him that his gorgeous young neighbor might be a mother. Finding out that she had kids—and not just the adorable twin boys but a baby girl, too—had scrambled his mind further.

Now that he knew about those children, it seemed wrong to admire the sweet curve of her buttocks in snug-fitting denim. And it was definitely depraved to let his gaze linger on the sway of those feminine hips—or to think about the fullness of breasts hugged by the soft blue knit cardigan she wore.

She might have been a mother, but that reality did nothing to alter the fact that she was also an incredibly attractive woman. Something about the sexy single mother next door stirred feelings inside of him that hadn't been stirred in a very long time. And while he was intrigued enough to want to explore those feelings, the kids were a definite complication.

Matt had dated a lot of women without letting them into his heart, but he had no defenses against the genuine friendliness and easy acceptance of children. Especially not when the loss of his son had left a gaping hole in his heart that ached to be filled.

"I know what you're thinking," Luke said, climbing back up onto the porch.

"You think so?"

His youngest brother nodded. "Yeah, she's a pleasure to look at. But she's got *complication* written all over her."

"I was only thinking that it was nice to finally meet my neighbor."

"You were thinking about asking her out," Luke accused.

"Maybe I was," he acknowledged.

Jack dropped an armload of painting tools at his feet. "Don't do it."

"Why not?" he asked, unwilling to be dissuaded.

"Slippery slope."

"You mean like an invitation to dinner might lead to a second date?" Matt didn't bother to disguise his sarcasm.

"And the next thing you know, you're walking down the aisle," Luke agreed.

"You went out with Becky McKenzie last week." He felt compelled to point this out. "But I don't see a ring on your finger."

"That's because when our little brother invites a woman to dinner, it's just an invitation to dinner," Jack explained.

"And maybe breakfast," Luke interjected with a grin.

"But when you ask a woman out on a first date..." Jack paused, his brow furrowing. "Well, we don't actually know what it means, because you haven't been out on a real date with anyone since Lindsay walked out on you."

"I've been out with plenty of women."

Luke shook his head. "You've hooked up with plenty of

women—but you haven't actually been in a relationship with any of them."

Now it was Matt's turn to frown, because he realized that what his brother had said was true.

"And this one comes with quite a bit of baggage," Jack noted.

"A three-piece set," Luke elaborated.

"You're reading way too much into this," Matt told them.

"I'm glad you're thinking about jumping back into the dating pool," Jack said. "But I don't get why you'd want to leap directly into the deep end when there are plenty of unencumbered beautiful women hanging out by the water."

Matt didn't know how to respond. He wasn't sure he could explain—even to himself—what it was about Georgia Reed that appealed to him. Or maybe he was afraid to admit that he'd fallen for the two little boys who had snuck over to look at the puppies even before he'd realized that his pretty blonde neighbor was their mother.

Since the breakup of his marriage, he'd been cautious about getting involved again. Having his heart trampled by his ex-wife was bad enough, he wasn't going to risk having it trampled by anyone else's children.

Not again.

Or so he'd thought—until Quinn and Shane raced into his backyard.

"I'm not looking for anything more than a chance to get to know my neighbor a little better," Matt insisted.

"So get to know her," Luke agreed. "But don't get involved with her. A relationship with someone who lives next door might seem convenient at first, but it can be a nightmare if things don't work out."

"Almost as bad as falling into bed with a woman who was supposed to be a friend," Jack said.

The statement was made with such conviction Matt was sure there must be a story behind it. But since he didn't want to discuss his personal life—or current lack thereof—he certainly wasn't going to grill his brothers about their respective situations.

"If you're lonely, you should think about getting a pet," Luke suggested.

"Like a puppy?" Matt asked dryly.

His brother grinned. "Man's best friend."

"A dog is too much of a commitment."

"Less than a woman and her three kids," Jack pointed out.

Which was a valid consideration, so Matt only said, "Are we going to spend all day sitting around and talking like a bunch of old women or are we going to paint this damn deck?"

"Since you put it that way," Luke said. "I guess we're going to paint the damn deck."

Chapter Two

After Pippa was changed and fed and the boys had helped make little pizzas for their lunch—using up all of the cheese and pepperoni and emptying the last jug of milk—Georgia knew a trip to the grocery store was in order. Since it was a nice day and Quinn and Shane seemed to have energy to burn, she decided they would walk rather than take the minivan.

The twins refused to ride in the double stroller anymore, insisting that they were too big to be pushed around like babies. Unfortunately, Georgia knew their determination and energy would last only so long as it took to reach their destination and not bring them home again, so she strapped Pippa into her carrier and dragged the wagon along beside her.

As she started down the driveway, she caught another glimpse of her hunky neighbor and his equally hunky brothers, and her pulse tripped again. The automatic physiological response surprised her. Since Phillip had died, all she'd felt was grief and exhaustion, so the tingles that skated through her veins whenever she set eyes on Matt Garrett weren't just unexpected but unwelcome.

She did *not* want to be attracted to any man, much less one she might cross paths with any time she stepped outside. But while her brain was firm in its conviction, her body wasn't nearly as certain.

Matt caught her eye and lifted a hand in greeting. She waved back, then quickly averted her gaze and continued on her way. It was bad enough that she'd caught herself staring—she didn't need her neighbor to be aware of it, too.

Of course, he was probably accustomed to women gawking in his direction. A man like that would be.

Not that she had a lot of experience with men like the Garrett brothers, but she knew their type. In high school, they would have been the most popular boys: the star athletes who had dated only the prettiest girls, the boys that other boys wanted to be and that all of the girls wanted to be with.

But not Georgia. She'd been too smart to fall into the trap of thinking that those boys would even look twice in her direction. And they never had. Not until Aiden Grainger sat down beside her in senior English and asked if she'd help out with the yearbook. Even then, she'd been certain he was only interested in her ability to correctly place a comma, and no one was more surprised than she when he walked her home after school one day and kissed her.

And with the first touch of his lips, she'd fallen for him, wholly and completely. They'd dated through the rest of senior year and talked about backpacking around Europe after graduation. Aiden wanted to see the world and Georgia wanted to do whatever he wanted to do so long as she got to be with him.

This willingness to sacrifice her own hopes and dreams in favor of his terrified her. It reminded her of all the times her life had been upended because her mother decided that she had to follow her heart to another city or another state—usually in pursuit of another man.

When Georgia was thirteen and starting her third new school in three years, she'd promised herself that she would never do the same thing. And now, barely five years later, she was preparing to throw away a scholarship to Wellesley College in order to follow some guy around Europe? No, she couldn't do it.

Aiden claimed that he was disappointed in her decision, but it turned out he wasn't disappointed enough to change his plans. He'd said he wanted to travel with her, but in the end, he wanted Europe more than he wanted her. And maybe Georgia wanted Wellesley more than she wanted him, because she went off to college and didn't look back.

But it had taken her a long time to get over Aiden, and a lot longer than that before she'd been willing to open up her heart again. And when she finally did, she'd lucked out with Phillip Reed.

Maybe theirs hadn't been a grand passion, but for almost ten years, he'd made her feel loved and comfortable and secure. It was all she'd ever wanted or needed.

So how was it that, after less than ten minutes, Matt Garrett had made her wonder if there might be something more? How was it that he'd stirred a passion inside of her that she'd never even known existed? And what was she supposed to do with these feelings?

Unable to answer any of these unnerving questions, she pushed them aside and led the kids into the grocery store.

When Matt decided to move, his real estate agent had repeated the same mantra: location, location, location. And Tina Stilwell had promised that this neighborhood scored top marks in that regard. There were parks, recreation facilities, a grocery store and schools in the immediate vicinity, with more shopping, restaurants and the hospital—where he worked as an orthopedic surgeon—just a short drive away. She hadn't mentioned the beautiful blonde next door, and

Matt wasn't sure how that information might have factored into his equation.

He hadn't necessarily been looking for a house—and he certainly wasn't looking for a new relationship. But he believed that real estate was a good investment and this house, in particular, had everything he wanted, not just with respect to location but amenities.

Jack had, logically, questioned why a single man needed four bedrooms and three bathrooms, forcing Matt to acknowledge that it was more space than he needed. He didn't admit—even to himself—that he had any residual hope of utilizing those extra bedrooms someday. Because he had a new life now—a new home and a new beginning, and he wasn't going to waste another minute on regrets or recriminations about the past. From this point on, he was going to look to the future.

But first, he had to cut the grass.

As he pushed the lawn mower across his yard, he kept casting surreptitious glances toward his neighbor's house, eager for any sign of Georgia Reed. He hadn't seen much of her in the past few days, and he knew she wasn't home now because the minivan was missing from her driveway, but that didn't stop him from checking every few minutes.

Thinking about what his brothers had said, he had to admit, albeit reluctantly, that it might not be a good idea to make a move on the woman next door. At least, not until he'd finished unpacking. If he moved too fast, she might think he was desperate. And he wasn't—but he was lonely.

Since his divorce, he'd had a few brief affairs but nothing more meaningful than that. He missed being in a relationship. He missed the camaraderie, the companionship and the intimacy. Not just sex—but intimacy. After a few unsatisfactory one-night stands, he'd recognized that there was a distinct difference.

He missed falling asleep beside someone he genuinely wanted to wake up with the next morning. He missed long conversations across the dinner table, quiet nights on the couch with a bowl of popcorn and a movie, and rainy Sunday mornings snuggled up in bed. He missed being with someone, being part of a couple, having a partner by his side to celebrate not just all of the national holidays but all of the ordinary days in between.

But even more than he missed being a husband, he missed being a father. For almost three years, his little boy had been the center of his life. But Liam had been gone for more than three years now, and it was past time that Matt accepted that and moved on.

With a sigh, he considered that maybe he should let Luke talk him into taking one of those puppies. At least then he wouldn't come home to an empty house at the end of a long day.

Glancing toward Georgia's house again, he was willing to bet that his neighbor didn't know what it meant to be lonely. With three kids making constant demands on her time, she probably didn't have five minutes to herself in a day.

No doubt the twins alone could keep her hopping, and she had the needs of an infant to contend with as well. Although he had yet to meet the baby girl, he found himself wondering what she looked like, if she had the same dark hair and dark eyes as her brothers (which he assumed they'd inherited from their father) or blond hair and blue eyes like her mother.

It had to be difficult for Georgia, being widowed at such a young age. Not that he actually knew how old she was, but if she'd passed her thirtieth birthday, he didn't think she'd done so very long ago. Which meant that she'd likely married when she was young and idealistic and head over heels in love—and that she was probably still grieving the loss of her husband. But even if she wasn't, Matt didn't imagine that she had any interest in—or energy for—a romance with her new neighbor.

A relationship with someone who lives next door might

seem convenient...but it can be a nightmare if things don't work out.

Luke was probably right. So Matt was going to take his brother's advice and step back. Which didn't mean he and Georgia couldn't be friends. Surely his brothers wouldn't have any objection to Matt being friends with the woman next door.

And it seemed obvious that the first step toward becoming friends was to be a good neighbor. He finished the last strip of his grass and pushed the mower over to Georgia's lawn.

Having never owned anything with a yard before, he wasn't sure how he would feel about the required maintenance and upkeep, but so far, he was enjoying the physical work. And mowing the lawn, being unable to hear anything but the rumble of the motor, was almost relaxing. Or it would have been if the hum and the vibration of the machine in his hands hadn't started him thinking about different hums and vibrations that he hadn't experienced in a very long time.

Yeah, it had definitely been too long since he'd been with a woman. Which brought him back to thinking about Georgia again. The neighbor who was, he reminded himself, strictly off-limits with respect to any kind of romance.

But while his mind might be willing to heed the warnings of his brothers, his hormones weren't entirely convinced. Especially when Georgia's van pulled into the driveway and his pulse actually skipped a beat.

As Georgia turned onto Larkspur Drive, she mentally reviewed her plans for the rest of the day. First and foremost was the long-neglected manuscript still on the dining room table. And when she finally got that manuscript finished, she would set Pippa up in her playpen on the deck while Georgia cut the grass. She still had mixed feelings about letting the boys play in the neighbor's yard, but she thought she might indulge them today, trusting they would keep safely out of the way in the tree house.

She hadn't seen much of Matt Garrett over the past few days, which made her realize how little she knew about him aside from his name. She didn't know where he worked or what he did, whether he was married or engaged or otherwise involved. Not that she was interested, just...curious.

And when she turned into her driveway and saw him pushing a lawn mower over the last uncut strip of grass in front of her house, her curiosity was piqued even further.

She parked her minivan, then opened the back door to let the twins scamper out before she unlatched Pippa's car seat. By the time she'd taken the baby into the house, he'd finished the lawn and was making his way toward her.

"Need a hand?" He gestured to the grocery bags in the back.

Georgia turned to respond, but the words dried up inside her mouth. His hair was tousled, his bronzed skin bore a light sheen of perspiration, and the gray T-shirt that molded to his broad shoulders and strong arms was damp with sweat. She'd always appreciated men who were more *GQ* than *Outdoorsman,* but she couldn't deny that there was something very appealing about *this* man.

She swallowed. "No, I've—"

Ignoring her protest, he reached into the vehicle for the remaining two bags.

She blew out a breath. "Okay. Thanks."

He grinned at her, and her knees actually went weak.

Something *very* appealing, indeed.

The first time she'd seen him up close, she'd been struck by his stunning good looks—and unnerved by her body's instinctive response to his blatant masculinity. But she'd managed to convince herself that she'd overestimated his appeal, that he couldn't possibly be as handsome or as sexy as she'd thought. Face-to-face with him now, she was forced to admit that, if anything, she'd *under*estimated his impact.

Those deep blue eyes were both warm and seductive, and

his exquisitely shaped mouth seemed to promise all sorts of wicked pleasure. Not that she was interested in seduction or pleasure; she didn't even have the energy for an innocent flirtation. But the pulsing of the blood in her veins proved that her body was only exhausted, not dead.

Matt followed her into the house and set the grocery bags on the counter.

"Can we come over to see the puppies?" Quinn asked.

Shane looked up at their neighbor, too, the plea in his gaze as earnest as his brother's question.

"The puppies aren't at my house today," Matt told them.

Their hopeful smiles dimmed.

"Where are they?"

"With my brother, Luke, at his clinic."

"He's the doggy doctor," Quinn reminded Shane.

"He's a doctor for all kinds of animals," Matt clarified.

"Maybe we could visit the puppies at the clinic," Quinn suggested.

"Not today," Georgia told him.

Shane pouted. "I want a puppy."

"Well, you got a baby sister instead."

"I'd rather have a puppy," Quinn grumbled.

Matt turned to hide his smile as he washed his hands at the sink. "Those puppies were kind of cute," he agreed. "But your sister is even cuter."

"Do you think so?" Quinn's tone was skeptical.

"Absolutely." He smiled at the baby still securely strapped into her car seat but directed his next words to Georgia. "Can I take her out of there?"

She hesitated. "If you want, but she doesn't have a lot of experience with strangers so she might..."

Her explanation trailed off when she saw that he already had Pippa out of her carrier.

Matt looked up. "She might what?"

"I was going to say 'fuss,'" she admitted. "But obviously she is doing anything but."

Instead, the little girl's big blue eyes were intently focused on Matt's face and her mouth was stretched into a wide, gummy grin that filled his heart so completely, his chest ached.

"She's a charmer," he said, tucking her carefully into the crook of his arm so that her head and neck were supported.

"She has her moments," her mother agreed.

"Mostly she cries," Quinn said.

"'Specially at night," Shane added.

Georgia's sigh confirmed it was true. "Colic."

He'd had his own experience with a colicky baby, and he winced sympathetically. "Are you getting any sleep?" he asked.

"A lot less since my mom went away," she admitted. "But I'm managing—if you disregard the fact that I'm falling behind on my work, housework and yard work."

Shane tugged on the hem of her shirt. "I'm hungry."

"I know, honey. I'll get your lunch as soon as I get the groceries put away."

"Gill cheez?"

She smiled. "You bet."

"I want twisty pasta," Quinn announced.

"You had pasta yesterday," she reminded him. "We're having grilled cheese today. But you can go put cartoons on TV while you're waiting for your lunch, if you want."

Apparently that was an acceptable compromise, as the boys both scampered off to the living room.

"But you're not falling behind with your kids," he said. "And that's what really matters."

The smile that curved her lips was both genuine and weary. "And thanks to you, I'm no longer as far behind with the yard work as I used to be."

He shrugged. "I was cutting my grass anyway."

She took a jug of 2% and a tub of yogurt out of the bag, found room for them in the fridge.

"You should try soy milk," he told her.

She lifted a brow. "Because you have futures in soybeans?"

He grinned. "Because colic can be caused—or aggravated—by an intolerance to the proteins in the cows' milk consumed by a nursing mother."

She crossed her arms over her chest. "How did you know I'm nursing?"

To his credit, he managed to keep his gaze on her face without his eyes even flickering in the direction of her very lush breasts. "No baby bottles in the drying rack or the fridge."

"Very observant," she noted. "And how do you know about the soy milk?"

"I read a lot."

She'd finished putting away her groceries and reached into the drawer under the oven for a frying pan. "I used to read," she told him. "Sometimes even for pleasure."

He smiled. "You will again—someday."

"I'll take your word for it." She retrieved the butter from the fridge. "But for now, we're getting through one day at a time."

"I'd say you're doing better than that. You've got three great kids, Georgia."

She started buttering slices of bread. "I wish you could be here to tell me that at 3:00 a.m." Then she realized how her words might be misconstrued, and her cheeks filled with color.

He knew she wasn't issuing an invitation, but he found himself wishing that he could find some way to help her out, to be the man she turned to when she needed someone, to be the one who could ease some of the fatigue from around her eyes and put a smile on her face. But those were very dangerous wishes. She wasn't his wife, her kids weren't his kids, and he had to stop wanting things that couldn't be.

"I only meant that it would be nice to have *someone* around to reassure me in the early hours of morning when I feel like crying right along with Pippa," she hastened to clarify.

"Sharing a burden makes it lighter," he agreed easily, and scribbled his phone number down on the notepad on the counter. "And if you ever do need a hand—with anything and at any time—give me a call."

"You've already done me a huge favor by cutting the grass." Butter sizzled as she dropped the first sandwich into the hot pan.

"I didn't know there was a limit on good deeds."

She smiled again, and though he could see the fatigue in her eyes, the curving of her lips seemed to brighten the whole room. "I don't mean to seem ungrateful—"

"I wouldn't say ungrateful so much as resistant."

"I lived in New York City for the past dozen years," she told him. "I wasn't even on a first-name basis with most of my neighbors, and the biggest favor any of them ever did for me was to hold the elevator."

"Obviously moving to Pinehurst has been a big adjustment."

"My mother told me it was a different world. She encouraged me to make conversation with people I don't know, and she chided me for locking the doors of my van when it's parked in the driveway."

"You lock the doors of your vehicle in your own driveway?" he asked incredulously.

"When I first moved to New York , I lived in a third-floor apartment in Chelsea. Two weeks later, I wandered down to the little coffee shop on the corner without securing the dead bolt and by the time I got back with my latte, the place had been completely cleaned out."

"I can see how an experience like that would make anyone wary," he admitted. "But around here, neighbors look out for one another."

"Says the man who just moved into the neighborhood," she remarked dryly, turning the sandwich in the pan.

He grinned. "But I grew up in Pinehurst and I've lived here most of my life."

"And probably quarterbacked the high school football team to a state championship in your senior year," she guessed.

"Actually, I was a running back," he told her.

"Yeah, 'cause that makes a difference."

She removed one sandwich from the pan and dropped in another. Then she cut the first into four triangles, divided them between two plates and set them on the breakfast bar. She reached into the cupboard above the sink for two plastic cups, then maneuvered past him to the fridge for a jug of milk.

Though she moved easily in completing tasks she had no doubt performed countless times before, he was suddenly cognizant of the fact that he was just standing around.

"I'm in your way," he noted, moving aside so that he was leaning against the far stool at the counter, the baby still tucked securely in the crook of his arm.

She shook her head as she half filled the cups with milk. "If you weren't holding Pippa, she'd be screaming her head off, wanting her lunch, and I'd be juggling her and burning the sandwiches."

As she called the twins to the kitchen, he glanced down at the baby who had, in fact, shoved her fist into her mouth and was gnawing intently on her knuckles.

"Well, as long as I'm being useful," he said, his wry tone earning him a small smile from Georgia, and a wide drooly one from the baby in his arms.

The quick patter of footsteps confirmed that the boys had heard their mother's call, and they eagerly climbed up onto the stools at the counter.

Georgia moved back to the stove and flipped the next sandwich out onto a plate. She sliced it in half, then surprised Matt by setting the plate on the counter in front of him.

"Milk?" she asked. "Or did you want something else? I've got iced tea or juice or soda."

"Milk is fine," he said. "But I didn't expect you to feed me."

"It's just a grilled cheese."

"Which is much more appetizing than the cold pizza in my fridge at home."

She shrugged. "I figured a sandwich is a small price to pay for lawn maintenance."

"You might get the hang of small-town living yet," he told her.

"I'm trying."

The fact that she was making an effort gave him confidence that their fledgling friendship could lead to something more.

And though Jack's and Luke's warnings still echoed in the back of his mind, they were easily drowned out by the pounding of his heart when Georgia smiled at him.

Chapter Three

Georgia waited until Matt's car was gone from his driveway before she okayed the boys' request to visit the neighbor's tree house. Over the past couple of weeks, they'd enjoyed several adventures in the treetop, but only when their new neighbor wasn't home.

It wasn't that she was avoiding Matt. Not exactly. There was just something about the man that set off warning bells in her head. Or maybe it was tingles in her veins.

He was friendly and great with the kids, and if not for the way her body hummed whenever he was near, she might have thought that they could be friends. But the sizzle of awareness was too powerful for her to be comfortable in his presence, so Georgia decided that it would be best to maintain a safe distance from him at all times—or at least until her post-pregnancy hormone levels were back to normal.

She carted Pippa over to the neighbor's backyard so that she could keep an eye on the boys while they played in the branches.

With the baby cooing happily in her playpen, Georgia settled in a folding lawn chair beside her. She smiled as she listened to the boys' conversation—or rather Quinn's animated chatter and Shane's brief responses. A few minutes later, she saw Shane's sneaker on the top step of the ladder.

"Be careful," she said, instinctively rising from her chair in the exact moment that his foot slipped off the next step. She was halfway to the tree, her heart lodged in her throat, when his body plummeted toward the ground.

Emergencies were par for the course for any doctor, and especially for one who worked in a hospital E.R. But when an emergency surgery was squeezed into a very narrow window between two scheduled procedures, it made an already long day seem that much longer.

After a quick shower, Matt decided to head to the cafeteria for a much-needed hit of caffeine. But then he saw Brittney—a much more effective mood booster than any jolt of java. He slung an arm across her shoulders and pressed his lips to the top of her head.

She, predictably, rolled her eyes. "A little professionalism, Dr. Garrett."

"My apologies, Miss Hampton," he said, not sounding the least bit apologetic.

Brittney Hampton was his former sister-in-law's only child and a student helping out in the E.R.—a co-op placement for which she'd applied without his knowledge, determined to secure the position on the basis of her interview and not because her uncle was a doctor on staff at the hospital. She was loving the experience, and he was pleased to see that she was so intently focused on the pursuit of her goals.

"Are you on a break?" he asked her.

She nodded. "Dr. Layton said I should take one now, while there's a lull in the E.R."

"A lull never lasts long," Matt agreed. "If you're heading to the cafeteria, can I buy you a cup of coffee?"

She made a face. "I hate coffee."

He smiled. "Hot chocolate? Coke?"

"Vitamin water?"

"Sold."

They settled at one of the tables by the window with their beverages.

"How was your morning?" Brittney asked him.

"In addition to the usual hip replacements, I put a plate and five screws in the ankle of a kid who took an awkward tumble on the soccer field."

She winced. "Sounds painful."

"Nah, we put him under so he didn't feel a thing."

She rolled her eyes. "I meant the tumble."

"I imagine it was," he agreed. "How was your morning?"

"I had a test on molecular genetics," she said.

"And?" he prompted.

She shrugged. "I think I did okay."

"So no worries that Northeastern is going to rescind their offer?" he teased.

"Not yet."

"Is Brayden going to Northeastern, too?"

"Brayden is old news," she told him.

"Oh. I'm…sorry?" Truthfully, he was relieved. On the few occasions that he'd met her boyfriend, he'd seemed like a nice enough kid but Matt had worried that the relationship with Brayden would distract Brittney from her studies and her ultimate goal of becoming a doctor like her uncle.

She smiled, at least a little. "It was a mutual decision."

"Then your heart isn't broken?"

"Not even bruised."

"Glad to hear it," he said.

"How's *your* heart?" she countered.

His brows lifted. "Do they have you working in cardiology now?"

She smiled again, but her eyes—when they met his—showed her concern. "Mom told me that Aunt Lindsay is having another baby."

"Yes, she is," he acknowledged, pleased that his voice remained level, betraying none of the emotions that churned inside of him whenever he thought about the family that his ex-wife now had with her new husband. He didn't resent the fact that Lindsay had everything he'd ever wanted, but he was painfully aware of how empty his own life was in contrast.

"You should get married again, too," Brittney said.

"Don't worry about me—I'm doing okay," he said. And it was true. Because he suddenly realized that, since moving in next door to Georgia Reed and her family, his life didn't seem quite so empty anymore.

"You need a family."

"I haven't given up on that possibility just yet."

"Mom was telling Grandma that you need a woman who can appreciate you for all of your good qualities," Brittney continued, "so I've been keeping my eyes open for—"

"I appreciate the thought, but the last thing I need is my sixteen-year-old ni—"

"*Seven*teen," she interjected. "Remember? You came by for cake and ice cream for my birthday last month."

"I remember," he assured her. In fact, he hadn't missed a single one of her birthdays in the past three years, and he was grateful that Brittney's mother had continued to include him in family events after the divorce. Of course, it probably helped that he and Kelsey had been friends long before he married her sister. "But the last thing I need is my *seven*teen-year-old niece trying to set me up."

"Well, I haven't found any candidates yet," she admitted. "Aside from my friend, Nina, who thinks you're really hot. But even I know how inappropriate that would be."

"And on that note," Matt said, pushing back his chair, "I think I should check in on my patient."

Brittney rose with him. "And I need to get back to the E.R."

But before she turned away, she gave him a quick hug.

He was as pleased as he was surprised by the impulsive gesture of affection. But it was the words she spoke—"You'll find someone, Uncle Matt"—that somehow shifted his thoughts to the beautiful widow living next door with her three children and made him wonder if maybe he already had.

Georgia didn't have a lot of experience with her kids and emergency rooms—thank God for small favors—but she knew that "the squeaky wheel gets the grease" was an adage that applied in hospitals as much as anywhere else. And when she finally managed to maneuver her family through the sliding doors, with Pippa fussing, Shane crying (and trying to hold a bag of now partially thawed frozen peas against his wrist), and Quinn shouting "Don't let him die!", she didn't even try to shush them. Or maybe she knew her efforts would be futile anyway.

After she gave the basic details of the incident and handed over her insurance information to the bored-looking clerk behind the desk, she was told—with a vague gesture toward the mostly empty seating area—to wait. But she didn't even have a chance to direct Quinn to an empty chair when a dark-haired girl in teddy-bear scrubs appeared with a wheelchair for Shane. Though the tag on the lanyard around her neck identified her as "Brittney" and confirmed that she was a member of the hospital staff, she didn't look to Georgia like she was old enough to be out of high school.

"I'm just going to take you for a walk down the hall to X-ray so that we can get some pictures of your arm," Brittney explained to Shane.

His panicked gaze flew to his mother. Georgia brushed a

lock of hair away from his forehead and tried not to let her own worry show.

"It's okay if your mom and your brother and sister want to come along, too," Brittney assured him. "Would that be better?"

Shane nodded.

Quinn shook his head vehemently. "I don't want Shane to get a X-ray. I wanna go home."

"We can't go home until a doctor looks at your brother's arm," Georgia reminded her son, holding on to her fraying patience by a mere thread. "And the doctor can't see what's inside his arm without an X-ray."

"*You* can make it better," Quinn insisted. "Kiss it and make it better, Mommy."

Georgia felt her throat tighten because her son trusted that it could be that simple, that she had the power to make it better because she'd always tried to do so. But they weren't babies anymore and Shane's injury wasn't going to be healed by a brush of her lips and a Band-Aid.

Just like when their father had died, there was nothing she could do to ease their pain. Nothing she could do to give them back what they'd lost or fill the enormous void that had been left in all of their lives.

"Unfortunately, that's not going to fix what's wrong this time," she told him.

"Does a X-ray…hurt?" Shane asked.

Brittney squatted down so that she was at eye level with the boy in the chair. "It might hurt a little when the tech positions your arm to take the picture," she admitted. "But it's the best way to figure out what to do next to make your arm stop hurting."

After a brief hesitation, Shane nodded. "Okay."

She smiled at him, then turned to Quinn and sized him up. "How old are you?"

"Four." He held up the requisite number of fingers proudly.

"Hmm." She paused, as if considering a matter of great importance. "I'm not sure if this will work."

"If what will work?" he immediately demanded.

"Well, hospital policy states that no one under the age of five is allowed to drive a wheelchair without a special license," she confided. "Do you have a license?"

Quinn shook his head.

Brittney rummaged in the pockets of her shirt and finally pulled out a small square of blue paper. "I have a temporary one here," she told him, and Georgia saw that the words TEMPORARY WHEELCHAIR LICENSE were printed in bold letters across the top of the paper. "And I can give it to you *if* you think you can steer the chair *slowly and carefully* all the way down the corridor to X-ray."

"I can do it," he assured her.

She looked to Georgia, who nodded her permission.

"Okay, then. But first I have to put your name on here—"

"Quinn Reed."

She uncapped a pen and carefully printed his name. "And the date?"

He looked to his mother for guidance on that one.

"May twenty-second," she supplied.

Brittney filled in the date, then recapped the pen and handed the "license" to Quinn. He studied the paper reverently for a moment before tucking it carefully into the pocket of his jeans and reaching up to take the handles of the chair.

"Just one warning," Brittney told him. "If you bump into anything or anybody, I'll have to revoke that license."

He nodded his understanding, and they set off toward the X-ray department.

Twenty minutes later, Brittney directed them into a vacant exam room with a promise that "Dr. Layton will be in shortly."

But one minute turned into two, and then five turned into

ten. And Pippa, already overdue for a feeding, made it clear—at the top of her lungs—that she would not be put off any longer.

Thankfully, Quinn seemed to have finally accepted that his brother wasn't in any immediate danger of dying, and he crawled up onto the hospital cot and closed his eyes. Shane was still crying, though there was only an occasional sob to remind her of the tears that ran down his cheeks. So Georgia eased Pippa out of the carrier and settled in a hard plastic chair to nurse the baby.

She tried to drape a receiving blanket over her shoulder, to maintain some degree of modesty, but Pippa was having none of it. Every time she tried to cover herself, her daughter curled her little fingers around the edge of the fabric and tugged it away, until Georgia gave up. Besides, she didn't imagine a nursing mother was either an unusual or scandalous sight in a hospital.

Of course, that was before Matt Garrett walked in.

In the few moments that Matt had taken to review the digital images before he tracked down the patient, he didn't manage to figure out why the name Shane Reed seemed familiar. Then he walked into exam room four and saw one little boy on the bed and an almost mirror image in the wheelchair parked beside it, and he realized Shane Reed was one half of the adorable twin sons belonging to his gorgeous neighbor. And sure enough, Georgia was seated beside the bed, nursing her baby girl.

The baby's tiny hand was curled into a fist and pressed against the creamy slope of her mother's breast, and her big blue eyes were wide and intent while she suckled hungrily. It was one of the most beautiful sights Matt had ever witnessed. And incredibly arousing.

"Mommy." It was Shane who saw him first, and he tapped his mother with his uninjured hand. "Mr. Matt's here."

Georgia's gaze shifted, locked with his and her pale cheeks filled with color.

"You're not Dr. Layton," she said inanely.

"Things are a little chaotic in the E.R. right now, so Dr. Layton asked me to take a look at Shane's X-ray."

Quinn sat up. "Are you a doctor, too?"

Matt nodded.

"You don't look like a doctor," he said accusingly.

"Quinn," his mother admonished.

But Matt was intrigued. "How does a doctor look?"

The little boy studied him for a minute. "Older," he decided. "With gray hair and glasses."

"I'm older than you," Matt pointed out.

"You still don't look like a doctor."

"Actually, I'm an orthopedist," he explained.

"See?" Quinn said triumphantly to his mother.

"An orthopedist *is* a doctor," she told him.

The boy looked to Matt for confirmation.

He nodded. "An orthopedist is a doctor who specializes in fixing broken bones."

"Is Shane—" Quinn swallowed "—broken?"

He managed to hold back a smile. "No, your brother isn't broken, but a bone in his arm is."

"I falled out of your tree house," Shane said quietly.

Matt winced. "All the way from the top?"

The little boy shook his head. "I missed a step on the ladder."

"And reached out with his arms to break his fall," Georgia finished.

He noted that she'd shifted Pippa to nurse from her other breast, and he quickly refocused his gaze on his patient. "And broke your arm, too," Matt told Shane. "Do you want to see the picture of your arm that shows the break?"

Shane sniffled, nodded.

Matt sat down in front of a laptop on the counter and tapped a few keys.

"This here is your radius—" he pointed with the tip of a pencil to the picture on the screen "—and this is your ulna."

Though the occasional tear slid down the boy's cheeks, his gaze tracked the movement of the pencil and he nodded his understanding.

"Do you see anything different about the two bones?"

"I do," Quinn immediately replied, as Shane nodded again.

"Well, since it's Shane's arm, I think we should let Shane tell us what's different," Matt said.

Quinn pouted but remained silent.

"What do you see, Shane?"

"The ra-di—" he faltered.

"Radius?" Matt prompted.

"It has a line in it."

"That line is the break, called a distal radius fracture."

"It hurts," Shane said, in a soft voice that was somehow both wounded and brave.

"I know it does," Matt agreed.

"Can you fix it?" Quinn asked. "You said you can fix broken bones."

He nodded. "Yes, I can, and I will."

Georgia tried to concentrate on what Matt was saying, but her mind was still reeling from the realization that her new neighbor wasn't just gorgeous and charming but a doctor, too. She couldn't have said why the information surprised her so much or what she'd expected.

While he was occupied with Shane, she took a closer look at him, her gaze skimming from his neatly combed hair to the polished loafers on his feet. This man certainly didn't bear any resemblance to the sexy gardener who had tended to her overgrown yard. If she'd taken a guess as to his occupation that day, she probably would have said that he was employed in some kind of physically demanding field, like construction work or firefighting. She certainly wouldn't have guessed that he was an M.D.

Maybe the Mercedes in his driveway should have been her first clue, though she'd never met a doctor who hadn't managed to reveal his profession within the first five minutes of an introduction. And she'd been living next door to the man for more than three weeks without him giving even a hint of his occupation. But as she watched *Dr.* Garrett now, she could see that he was completely in his element here.

As he explained the process of casting a broken bone, he used simple words that the boys could understand. Despite his careful explanation, though, Quinn remained wary.

"Is Shane going to die?" he asked, obviously terrified about his brother's potential fate.

Though Georgia instinctively flinched at the question, the doctor didn't even bat an eye.

"Not from a broken arm," he assured him.

Shane looked up, his dark eyes somber. "Do you promise?"

She felt her own eyes fill with tears when she realized that the question wasn't directed to her but to Matt. Which made perfect sense, since he was the doctor. But it was the first time since Phillip had died that either of the twins had sought reassurance from anyone but their mother, and emotionally, it cut her to the quick.

"I absolutely promise," he said.

And Shane's hesitant nod confirmed that he'd accepted the man's word.

"Can I ask you a question now?" Matt asked.

Shane nodded again.

"What's your favorite color?"

"Blue."

"Then we'll put a blue cast on your arm," the doctor announced, and earned a small smile from his patient.

He left the room for a few minutes, then came back with

Brittney and an older woman. The gray-haired nurse helped lift and maneuver Shane's arm while the doctor applied the cast and Brittney looked on, observing and providing a running commentary of the process to entertain the twins. When it was done, Matt tied a sling over Shane's shoulder and explained that it would help keep the arm comfortable and in place.

"Do you use your right hand or your left hand when you eat?" Brittney asked Shane.

"This one," he said, lifting his uninjured hand.

"Do you think you could handle an ice cream sundae?"

Shane nodded shyly, then looked to his mother for permission.

"They would love ice cream," she admitted to Brittney, reaching for her purse.

The girl waved a hand. "It's on Dr. Garrett—part of the service."

Matt passed her a twenty-dollar bill without protest.

"Does my wheelchair driver still have his license?"

Quinn pulled the paper out of his pocket.

"Then let's go get ice cream."

"Thanks, Britt," said Matt with a smile.

Georgia had mixed feelings as she watched her boys head out with the young nurse. They were growing up so fast, but they would always be her babies as much as the little one still in her arms.

"She's been wonderful," she said to Matt now. "I don't know that I would have survived this ordeal without screaming if she hadn't been able to engage the boys."

"It can't be easy, juggling three kids on your own on even a normal day."

"What is a normal day?"

He smiled at that. "I'm not sure I would know, but I'm sure it's not strapping three kids into car seats for a trip to the hospital."

"Mrs. Dunford did offer to look after Pippa and Quinn so I didn't have to bring them along but—" She knew there was no reason to feel embarrassed talking to a doctor about a perfectly natural biological function that women had been performing since the beginning of time, but that knowledge didn't prevent a warm flush of color from rising in her cheeks again. "But the baby was almost due for a feeding and Quinn was absolutely terrified at the thought of his brother going to the hospital."

"He has a phobia about hospitals?" he asked.

"They both do," she admitted.

"Any particular reason?"

She nodded. "Because their father—my husband—was in the hospital when he died."

"That would do it," he agreed.

"It was a heart attack," she explained. "He recognized the symptoms and called 9-1-1, but the damage was too severe. All the boys know is that he was alive when they put him in the ambulance and dead at the hospital."

"Now they think anyone who goes to the hospital is going to die," he guessed.

She nodded again. "I've tried to explain that it wasn't the doctor's fault—that it wasn't anybody's fault—but they don't seem to believe me."

"Which one is Mrs. Dunford?"

She smiled. "Across the street. Always outside at 7:00 a.m. in her housecoat, watering her flowers. She has a magic touch with geraniums."

"And gingersnap cookies," he said.

"She baked you cookies?"

"She wanted to welcome me to the neighborhood."

"More likely she wanted to set you up with her granddaughter."

"Then she should have gone for chocolate chip—they're my absolute favorite."

"I'll be sure to let her know."

He shook his head. "I'd prefer to get my own dates—although even Brittney thinks I need some help in that regard."

"Brittney—the nurse who looks like she's fifteen?"

"She's seventeen."

"Then she's not a nurse?"

He laughed. "More like pre-pre-med. Actually, Brittney's a high school co-op student who also happens to be my niece."

"She's been fabulous with the boys."

"She plans to specialize in pediatric medicine."

"That's quite an ambition."

"She's very determined. And she's one of the most sought-after babysitters in town."

"I'll keep that in mind if I ever find myself in need of one," she promised, certain Brittney would have graduated from medical school before that would ever happen.

So she was more than a little surprised when Matt said, "How about Friday night so I can take you out to dinner?"

Chapter Four

For a minute, she just stared at Matt as if he'd spoken in a foreign language. And with every second that ticked away during that interminable minute, he wondered if he should rescind his impulsive invitation.

He wasn't usually the impulsive type, a truth that was proven by the fact that he'd kept the condo he'd lived in with his wife and child for three years after they'd gone rather than take a hit on the downturned real estate market. Or maybe he just hadn't been ready to move on until now.

But he was ready now. And if Georgia agreed to go out with him—even just once for dinner—it would hopefully convince his niece to put her matchmaking efforts on hold.

"Are you asking me out…on a date?"

Except that her question, along with the skepticism in her voice, made him question whether he truly was capable of getting his own dates.

It can be a nightmare if things don't turn out.

He ignored the echo of Luke's words in the back of his

mind. While he trusted that his brother had his best interests at heart and believed that there was some legitimacy to his warning, Matt couldn't deny the instinct that was urging him to get to know Georgia a whole lot better.

"Let's not put a label on it," he said instead.

"So it's not a date?"

"It isn't anything until you say yes."

She considered for another few seconds, then shook her head. "I can't."

"You can't have dinner with a friend? A neighbor?"

"I can't leave my kids with a stranger—even if she is one of the most sought-after babysitters in town."

But he thought that, for just a minute, she'd been tempted.

"Quinn and Shane seem to like her just fine," he pointed out.

"She's been great with the twins," she said again. "But Pippa is another story. There are certain things that no one but Mommy can do for her."

Okay, he didn't need to be hit over the head. At least, not more than once. And if his gaze automatically dropped to her breasts, well, he made a valiant effort to yank it away again.

Not so quickly that she didn't notice—as was attested by the color flooding her cheeks.

"Okay, then, how about dinner at my place so you're not too far away if you're needed?"

"Look, I appreciate the invitation, but I'm doing okay. You don't have to feel sorry for me because I'm on my own with three kids."

"Is that what you think—that I feel sorry for you?"

"I don't know what to think," she admitted. "But it's the only explanation I can imagine that makes any sense."

"Maybe it did occur to me that a few hours away from your responsibilities might be appreciated," Matt allowed. "But I don't feel sorry for you. In fact, I think you're lucky to have three beautiful children, and that they're lucky to have a mother so obviously devoted to them." Because he knew from firsthand experience that there was nothing quite like the bond between a parent and child—and that nothing else could fill the void when that bond was broken.

"I am lucky," she said softly. "Although I don't always focus on how very lucky—and I don't always know how to respond to unexpected kindness."

"You could respond by saying you'll come to my place for dinner on Friday."

She shook her head, but she was smiling. "You're persistent, aren't you?"

"That's not the response I was looking for," he reminded her.

"I'll come for dinner on Friday," she finally agreed. "*If* Brittney is available—and willing—to watch the kids."

"Is seven o'clock good?"

"Shouldn't you check with the babysitter first?"

"Brittney will make herself available," he assured her.

"Then seven o'clock should be fine," Georgia said.

"Any food allergies or aversions?"

She shook her head.

"Favorite food?"

She smiled. "Anything I don't have to cook."

It was a long night for Georgia.

She gave Shane some children's acetaminophen to take the edge off of the pain, but she could do nothing to combat his frustration. He was usually a tummy sleeper, and he didn't like having to stay on his back with his injured arm elevated on a pillow, even if it was what "Dr. Matt" had recommended.

And she didn't have any better luck settling Quinn. While he'd been happy enough to wheel his brother around the hospital and indulge in ice cream, neither activity had succeeded in completely alleviating his worry about his twin.

But aside from checking on Shane and reassuring Quinn

and nursing and pacing with Pippa, what really kept Georgia awake through the night was second-guessing her agreement to have dinner with her sexy new neighbor.

He was a genuinely nice man who was wonderful with her kids, and if those were the only factors to consider, Georgia wouldn't have hesitated to accept his invitation. But Matt Garrett made her feel things she hadn't felt in a very long time—if ever before—and the stirring of those unexpected feelings made her wary.

Her mother had always said that falling in love was kind of like jumping into a pool without testing the water. And there was no doubt that Charlotte had always enjoyed that crazy sense of plunging into the unknown. Georgia had never been the type to leap without looking—she liked to gauge the temperature first and ease in slowly.

And that was the perfect analogy for her relationship with Phillip. She'd loved her husband, but their affection had grown over time along with their relationship. They'd started out as friends who'd shared common interests and values—and a mutual distrust of romance. Phillip had been engaged previously, but that relationship had ended when he found his fiancée in bed with his cousin. Georgia had, as a result of her mother's numerous relationships more so than her own experience, mostly steered clear of any romantic entanglements.

But Phillip had been as persistent as he was charming, and one date had led to another until, before Georgia knew what was happening, they were exchanging vows. They'd had a good relationship, a solid marriage. They'd been compatible enough, even if the earth hadn't trembled when they made love, and she had sincerely loved him.

When they'd decided to get married, she'd had no reservations. It wasn't that she couldn't live without him so much as she didn't want to—he was her best friend, the one person she knew she could always rely on, and the one person she always felt comfortable with.

She didn't feel the least bit comfortable around Matt Garrett.

She was thirty-one years old and a mother of three children, and she didn't have the first clue about what to do with these feelings that he stirred inside of her. She wished, for just a minute, that Charlotte was here so that she could talk to her about this inexplicable attraction. Four marriages—and four divorces—had given her mother a lot of experience with love—and heartbreak.

Except that Georgia didn't need to talk to Charlotte to know what her advice would be. "Go for it. Have fun—and make sure you have orgasms. Life's too short to fake it."

She smiled, almost hearing the echo of her mother's voice in her mind even as she chided herself for jumping the gun. After all, just because the man had invited her over for dinner didn't mean he was looking for anything more than that. Just because her heart pounded wildly inside her chest whenever he was near didn't guarantee that he felt the same attraction.

"I'll be glad when your Gramma's home tomorrow," she said to her daughter. Not that she expected her mother would be able to put the situation in perspective for her, but she would help out with the kids so Georgia could get some sleep. Because after more than a week of serious sleep deprivation capped off by an unexpected trip to the emergency room, she was starting to feel more than a little frazzled. But she was confident she could handle things on her own for twenty-four more hours.

The first few weeks after Pippa's birth had been pure bliss. The baby had slept and nursed and cried very rarely, and Georgia had been completely enthralled with her. And then, around four weeks, Pippa had started to get fussy. She still slept and nursed frequently, but the sleeping was for shorter periods of time, the nursing more frequent, and the crying much louder and longer.

After a thorough checkup, Dr. Turcotte had announced

that there was absolutely nothing wrong with her aside from "a touch of colic." He'd been sympathetic but unable to help. And though Charlotte had offered to cancel her annual trip with "the girls," Georgia couldn't imagine letting her do it. Because if she'd accepted that offer, it would be like admitting that she couldn't handle her own baby. Besides, Charlotte had already done so much for her daughter and her grandchildren.

When everything had started to fall apart in Georgia's life, her mother hadn't hesitated to invite her to come home. Not that Pinehurst, New York, had ever actually been *her* home. In fact, Charlotte had only settled in the picturesque upstate town about half a dozen years earlier, long after Georgia was living and working in New York City. But Georgia hadn't needed a familiar environment so much as she'd needed her mother. As she needed her now.

She was passing the kitchen when the phone rang, and she grabbed for the receiver automatically, forgetting for a moment that she didn't need to worry about the noise waking the baby because Pippa was already awake and snuggled happily—at least for the moment—in her carrier.

Georgia recognized her mother's voice immediately. "Hey, Mom, I was just talking to Pippa about you."

"How is my beautiful grandbaby girl?" Charlotte asked.

She always sounded upbeat, but Georgia thought she sounded even more so today. Not that it took much to make her mother happy—something as simple as winning a couple of hands at the blackjack table or scoring front-row seats to see Wayne Newton could be responsible for her joyful mood.

"She seems content enough right now," Georgia said, not wanting to let her mother know how difficult the last few days had been.

"Oh, I miss my grandbabies so much," Charlotte said. "Have you been givin' them all big hugs and kisses from me every day?"

"I have," she assured her mother. "But they're looking

forward to getting them directly from you when you come home tomorrow."

"Well, that's actually why I was callin'," Charlotte began, and Georgia felt a sinking sensation in the pit of her belly. "There's been a little bit of a change in my plans."

"What kind of change?" She tried to keep her voice light and borrow the brave face her mother always wore.

"I met someone." The excitement fairly bubbled over in Charlotte's voice again. "Oh, honey, I didn't think I would ever fall in love again. I certainly didn't expect it. I mean, I've already been so lucky in love—"

Lucky? Only Charlotte Warring-Eckland-Tuff-Masterton-Kendrick would think that four failed marriages somehow added up to lucky. On the other hand, her effervescent personality and unfailing optimism were no doubt two of the qualities that continued to draw men to her, in addition to the fact that she looked at least a decade younger than her fifty-four years.

Okay, Georgia thought, trying to be rational about this. Her mother had met someone. She certainly didn't have any philosophical objection to Charlotte having a romantic relationship—not really. But she did object to her mother, or anyone for that matter, believing that she'd fallen in love with a man she couldn't have known for more than a handful of days.

"—but the minute our eyes met across the baccarat table," Charlotte continued, "I felt a jolt as if I'd just stuck my finger in a socket."

Georgia had to smile at that. "I'm glad you're having a good time—"

"The *best* time," Charlotte interjected. "And after the ceremony last night, Trigger got us upgraded to the honeymoon suite, and I swear, I drank so much champagne my head is still spinnin'."

Right now, Georgia's head was spinning, too. Ceremony? Honeymoon suite? *Trigger?*

"Mom," she said, attempting to maintain a rational tone in the hope that it would calm the panic rising inside her. "Are you telling me that you married this guy?"

"Honey, when love comes knockin' on the door, you don't just open up, you grab hold with both hands and drag it inside."

Georgia banged her forehead softly against the wall.

"So yes," Charlotte finally answered her question. "I am now, officially, Mrs. Trigger Branston."

"His name is really Trigger?"

"Oh, his real name's Henry," she told her daughter. "But they call him Trigger 'cause he's so quick on the draw."

"Quick on the draw?" she echoed, fingers crossed that this whole conversation was some kind of bizarre waking dream induced by her own mental and physical exhaustion.

"With his gun," Charlotte clarified. "He's a *bona fide* member of the Cowboy Fast Draw Association and World Fast Draw Association and he's won all kinds of contests."

"That's…um…impressive?"

"You bet your cowboy boots it is," Charlotte said.

Georgia didn't remind her mother that the only boots she owned were of the snow-shoveling kind. What would be the point?

"So…this is what he does for a living?" she pressed.

Her mother laughed. "Of course not—the gun-slingin' thing is just a hobby. Trigger's ranch keeps him too busy for it to be anything else."

"Where is this ranch?"

"In southwestern Montana."

"You're moving to *Montana?*"

"Well, he can hardly bring the sheep and goats all the way to upstate New York," Charlotte pointed out.

Sheep and goats?

Georgia didn't want to imagine. Besides, she had a more pressing concern. "What are your plans for the house here?"

"Oh, I haven't even thought about that. But naturally you and my grandbabies can stay there as long as you want."

The statement was typical of her mother—equal parts impulsive and generous. And while Georgia appreciated the offer, her main reason for packing up her family and moving them to Pinehurst was that Charlotte was there.

But she bit her tongue. How could she do anything else when her mother sounded so happy and proud? What right did she have to begrudge her mother a new life just because her own had completely imploded?

So even while her eyes burned with tears, she said, "Congratulations, Mrs. Branston."

Her mother's laughter bubbled over the line. "I knew you'd be happy for me, baby girl."

And she was—at least, she really wanted to be. Because Charlotte Warring-Eckland-Tuff-Masterton-Kendrick-Branston had the biggest heart in the world and she deserved to be happy. But when Trigger Branston trampled all over that big heart with his Montana cowboy boots, Georgia thought ominously, he was going to answer to her.

Or maybe she was being too cynical. The fact that none of her mother's four previous marriages had worked out didn't mean that this one wouldn't. And really, who was she to judge? Just because Georgia didn't want to follow in Charlotte's footsteps didn't give her the right to condemn her mother's choices.

Maybe she had no interest in a steamy romance or a hunky man because she only wanted a few hours of sleep—preferably dreamless sleep. Because over the past couple of weeks, it seemed as if every time she closed her eyes, she couldn't help but dream about the sexy doctor next door.

Matt was wrapping potatoes in foil when the doorbell rang. Since it was just past six o'clock and, therefore, too early to be Georgia, he decided to ignore it. When he heard the door open and heavy footsteps in the foyer, he knew it had to be one of his brothers. An assumption that was proven accurate when Jack strolled into the kitchen.

His brother automatically reached for the handle of the fridge. "Do you want a beer?"

"No, thanks. But help yourself," Matt said dryly.

Jack did so and deftly twisted the cap off of a long-neck green bottle, his gaze zeroing in on the package of steaks. "Either you're really hungry or I picked the right night to stop by for dinner."

"You're *not* staying," Matt told him.

Undeterred, his brother dropped into a chair. "Why—you got a hot date or something?"

"As a matter of fact, I do."

Jack's bottle thunked down on the table. "You really have a date?"

"Is that so hard to believe?"

"Actually, yes."

Matt scowled as he tossed the foil-wrapped potatoes into the preheated oven. "I date."

His brother shook his head. "You've never invited anyone back to your place."

"It felt strange when I was still at the condo," Matt admitted. "Being with someone else there."

"Then you should have moved out of that place three years ago."

"Maybe I should have," he acknowledged. He'd known, long before the divorce was final, that his marriage was over. But he'd still been reluctant to leave the home that held so many memories of the little boy who had been his son for far too brief a time.

"So who is she?"

Jack's question drew him back to the present. "No one you know. Now finish your beer and get out."

"Maybe I should hang around to get to know her," his brother teased. "Maybe she'll like me better than you."

"You have enough women falling at your feet without homing in on mine."

Jack's brows lifted. "Is she? Your woman, I mean."

"It's a first date, Jack." And then, in a not-so-subtle effort to change the topic of conversation, he asked, "So what's going on with you?"

His brother shook his head. "It's the mom, isn't it? That's why you're trying to change the topic."

"I'm just curious as to why you're dateless on a Friday night," Matt hedged.

"Things were getting a little intense with Angela, so I decided to take a break from the dating scene for a while."

"I thought you really liked Angela."

"I did," he agreed. "And then I noticed that she was starting to stockpile bridal magazines."

"Someday you'll find the right woman and take the plunge again," Matt assured him.

Jack shook his head and reached for his beer. "I like to think I learned from my mistakes. One failed marriage is enough for me."

"Did you hear that Kelly Cooper's moving back home?"

"Yeah, I heard."

"I just wondered if that might be the real reason you decided to end things with Angela."

"Our youngest brother was the one who was always tight with the girl next door."

Matt couldn't help but laugh at that. "Because they were best friends—not because there was any kind of romantic connection."

Jack shrugged, but Matt knew that his brother's efforts to appear unconcerned only proved that he cared more than he wanted anyone to know.

"I always wondered why she never came home," Matt

mused now. "We all knew she was excited about going to school in Chicago, but no one expected that she would go from Chicago to Dallas to Seattle, or that she would stay away for so long."

"I'm sure she had her reasons."

"Would you be one of those reasons?"

Before Jack could respond, a knock sounded at the back door.

"I guess that's my cue," he said, picking up his almost-empty bottle to finish it off.

Matt didn't protest. The last thing he wanted was his brother hanging around all night. But he refused to let Jack off the hook so easily. "We'll get back to this," he promised.

But apparently Jack wasn't letting him off the hook, either, because instead of heading out the front—the same way he'd come in—he went to the back door as Matt was opening it to his guest.

"Hello, Georgia," Jack said.

"Oh, hi." She seemed taken aback by the other man's presence. "Jack, right?"

He smiled, pleased that she'd remembered his name. "It's nice to see you again."

"Jack was just on his way out," Matt said pointedly.

His brother shook his head. "I'm not in any huge rush," he denied.

Georgia's gaze shifted from Matt to Jack and back again. "Am I interrupting?"

"No, *you* were invited," Matt reminded her. "*He's* interrupting."

"He's right," Jack acknowledged. "And I promise I won't stay for long. I just wanted to meet my brother's mystery date."

"I didn't know that I was a mystery—or that this was a date," Georgia admitted.

"It's just a friendly dinner," Matt affirmed, shooting a

warning glance at his brother. "Did you want something to drink? I've got sparkling water or juice or—"

"Water would be great," Georgia said. "Thanks."

But before he even had a chance to pour her drink, Matt's pager went off.

He swore silently, but he couldn't ignore it. Not wanting the night to be a complete write-off for Georgia, he reluctantly left Jack in charge.

Then Matt headed toward the hospital, already devising a plan to secure a second date—and hopefully a first kiss.

Chapter Five

Georgia was disappointed that Matt had to cancel their plans to go to the hospital, but she understood. She didn't understand why he'd insisted that she stay to enjoy the dinner he'd promised her, and she didn't know how to decline Jack's offer to barbecue without sounding rude. Her only hope was that Pippa would wake up and pitch such a fit next door that Brittney would call and demand that Georgia return home.

Of course, her cell phone remained stubbornly silent.

"Looks like Matt's taken care of everything," Jack told her, returning with the plate of steaks from the grill. "There's a green salad, baked potatoes and dinner rolls."

"He didn't have to go to so much trouble," Georgia said, feeling more than a little guilty that he wouldn't get to enjoy the meal himself. "I would have been thrilled with a burger."

"Obviously my brother thinks you're worth the trouble," he said.

Despite the compliment implicit in the words, something in Jack's voice warned Georgia that he wasn't so sure.

He set a steak on her plate. "Well done."

"I like my steak medium."

"Matt told me to cook it all the way through to ensure there's no risk of any bacteria."

Her smile was wry. "Does he try to take care of everyone?"

Jack dropped a spoonful of sour cream onto his baked potato. "He and Luke both—it's the nurturing-doctor thing."

"What's your thing?" Georgia wondered.

He grinned. "I'm the heartless lawyer."

She shook her head. "I don't believe that."

"I have a law degree to prove it."

"It's not the educational qualifications that I doubt—it's the claim of heartlessness."

"There are more than a few women in town, including my ex-wife, who would assure you it's true."

"You're close to, and protective of, your brothers," she noted.

He didn't deny it.

"And for some reason, you disapprove of Matt and I being friends."

"I don't disapprove of your friendship," he assured her.

"But?" she prompted.

"But—and I know Matt would kill me for saying this—he's vulnerable."

"And you think I'm going to take advantage of him in some way?"

"I don't know what to think," Jack admitted. "Because I don't know you."

"That's fair," she acknowledged. "Would it reassure you if I said that I'm not in the market for a husband or a father for my children?"

"Not really."

"Why not?"

"Because I know my brother and he doesn't give up on anything he wants."

"And you think he wants me?"

"I know he does," Jack told her. "Because he called dibs."

She set down her water glass. "Excuse me?"

"The day he moved in—the first time he saw you on the porch—he warned the rest of us to back off."

She wasn't sure whether to be amused or insulted. "I would think the three kids would be warning enough."

He shrugged. "It's all about balancing pros and cons. We're guys and you're hot—for most of our species, those factors outweigh everything else."

"I'm not sure how to respond to that," she admitted, blushing. "Thank you?"

"It was a compliment," he said, and grinned again. "And you're welcome."

"But I do think you're misreading the situation between your brother and me."

"I doubt it."

"Even if he might have been interested when we first met, I'm sure the brief interactions he's had with my kids since then have cured him of any romantic notions."

"If you really believe that, you don't know Matt at all."

"I'd be the first person to admit that I don't," she told him.

"Which is probably why he invited you for dinner tonight," Jack noted.

"He's been incredibly helpful and generous."

"Don't kid yourself into thinking that he doesn't want to see you naked."

"You are blunt, aren't you?"

He shrugged easily. "I believe in telling it the way it is. But as much as he does want to get you naked, I know he could easily grow to care for you, too, and that makes the situation even more complicated."

"I'm not looking for a relationship," Georgia said.

"Sometimes we don't know what we want until it's right in front of us."

"That's quite the philosophical statement from a man who claims to value a woman on the basis of her 'hotness.'"

He flashed that quick grin again. "I can't be philosophical and shallow?"

She sliced off a piece of steak. "I think you're not nearly as shallow as you want people to believe."

Jack just shrugged, but Georgia suspected there were a lot more layers to each of thc Garrett brothers than they let anyone see. Which was just one more reason for her to steer clear of all of them.

Her life was complicated enough right now without adding a man to the mix, especially one who had the potential to send her life—and her heart—into a tailspin, as she suspected Matt Garrett had already started to do.

Matt had just finished pouring his first cup of coffee Saturday morning when his youngest brother walked in.

"What are you doing here?" he asked Luke.

"Jack told me about your date last night."

"It wasn't much of a date," Matt admitted, pouring a second cup of coffee for his brother and adding a generous splash of cream.

"Yes, he said that you were saved by the bell—or at least your pager." Luke accepted the proffered cup.

"What is it, exactly, that I was supposedly saved from?" Matt asked. "A few hours in the company of a beautiful woman?"

"Let's put aside the fact that she's a beautiful woman—and your neighbor—for just a minute," Luke suggested, "and focus on the fact that she has three kids."

"I like kids."

"I know—and I saw the look on your face when those two little boys scampered across your backyard."

"What look was that?" Matt lifted his cup to his lips again.

"Pain. Regret. Longing."

He snorted. "Really? You got all that from one look?"

Luke shrugged. "I know you, and I know what you've been through."

"Ancient history," he said dismissively. Because while the scars from his failed marriage and the loss of his son had not completely healed, they had started to fade—and even more quickly since he'd met Georgia and her kids.

"Your marriage is history and Liam is gone," his brother agreed. "But I doubt you've given up on wanting a family."

"If we're going to start talking about our feelings, I'm going to need something a little stronger than coffee," Matt told him.

"I get that you're lonely," Luke continued as if his brother hadn't spoken. "But zeroing in on the first woman who crosses your path—"

"Georgia's hardly the first woman to cross my path in the past three years," Matt chided.

"But she's the first one you've invited over for a home-cooked dinner."

"It was a couple of steaks on the grill, not a six-course meal."

Luke just stared at him over the rim of his mug.

"Okay," he finally acknowledged. "So I like her. What's the big deal?"

"The big deal is that you're setting yourself up for heartbreak all over again. She was married to another man—presumably because she was in love with that other man—and her kids are that other man's kids."

"The situation is not the same," Matt denied, though he could understand why his brother might worry about the similarities. "Georgia is a widow."

"Which doesn't mean she's not still in love with her husband."

He knew it was true, but he also knew that there was a

definite crackle in the air whenever he was near Georgia, and he didn't believe he was the only one who felt it.

"I'm only suggesting that you expand your horizons," Luke said now.

Matt eyed him warily. "Expand my horizons—how?"

"Come out to Maxie's with us tonight."

"Maxie's? Are you kidding?" While he and his brothers had frequented the popular dance club when they were younger, the loud music and louder women didn't appeal to him anymore.

"It might be just what you need," Luke said.

"I doubt it."

"Come anyway," his brother cajoled. "If you don't have a good time, I'll back off and not say another word about your infatuation with your neighbor."

Matt snorted his disbelief.

"And I'll buy the beer."

"Well, in that case…"

Matt spent the afternoon framing the unfinished basement to divide the space into individual rooms. Although the house already had a lot of space, he thought it would be convenient to have a home gym so that he didn't have to head out whenever he wanted some exercise. And until the room was ready, he figured the construction itself was a pretty good workout.

The physical labor occupied his hands but not his mind, and he found himself wondering what Georgia was doing, if the twins were behaving, if Pippa was napping. He remembered those first few months with Liam, how he and Lindsay had struggled to meet the baby's needs and establish some routines. His life had never been quite as chaotic as it had been back then, and he was surprised to realize that he missed it. Of course, spending time with his neighbors had given him brief glimpses of that pandemonium again, and spending time in close proximity to Georgia had stirred his hormones into a frenzy. He hammered the final nail into a board and tried to push those thoughts from his mind.

He was covered in sweat and sawdust and heading for the shower—prompted by the text message Luke had sent to remind him of their plans (because his brother knew Matt would forget, or at least claim he'd forgotten, without such a reminder)—when the bell rang.

Since his brothers had already proven that they had no qualms about walking right in, he let himself hope that it might be Georgia at the door. And while a quick glance through the sidelight revealed a pair of shapely, tanned legs, the hem of a short skirt and a pair of slender arms wrapped around an enormous ceramic pot from which towered a plant with lots of glossy, green leaves, his hopes were dashed.

He opened the door, made a show of looking around the greenery. "I really need to find a landscaper who can deal with these weeds. They're out of control."

"It's not a weed, it's a schefflera."

"Kelsey?" He parted some branches, peeked between them. Maybe she wasn't the woman who had preoccupied so many of his thoughts over the past few weeks, but she was one of his best friends, and he was genuinely happy to see her. "Are you in there?"

His former sister-in-law shoved the pot at his midsection, causing the air to whoosh out of his lungs. "Happy housewarming."

He maneuvered back through the door and carefully set the pot on the floor. "It's a killer plant," he said, after he'd managed to catch his breath again. "Although chances are, I'll kill it first."

"It's low maintenance," she assured him. "But don't leave it by the door in the winter. And it needs lots of light, but not direct sunlight."

"Low maintenance like most women are low maintenance," he grumbled.

She just smiled as she kissed his cheek, then moved past him and into the foyer. "This is a great house."

"Why do you sound so surprised?"

"Because it's a house—and nothing at all like your condo. Even the furniture's different."

"I was ready for a fresh start."

She nodded, understanding, and continued toward the kitchen. "I'm sorry I didn't get a chance to stop by sooner," she said. "One of the cruise lines is having a summer sale and things have been crazy at the office."

"You know, a ticket for a cruise would have been a better housewarming gift than a plant."

"Except that you don't take vacations," she reminded him. "In fact, I don't think you've gone on a holiday since…"

"Since my honeymoon?" he guessed, when her words trailed off.

She winced. "I'm sorry."

"The divorce has been final for three years," he pointed out.

"I know," she admitted.

The sympathy and worry in her deep brown eyes made him realize that he'd given her cause for concern in those three years because he hadn't taken any concrete steps to prove that he was moving on with his life. Hopefully seeing him in his new home would prove to her that he was doing so now.

He opened the refrigerator, peered inside. "Beer, wine, soda, juice?"

"Juice sounds good."

He pulled out the jug of orange juice, filled a tall glass, grateful that she'd dropped the topic of his ex-wife—her sister.

"Am I going to get the grand tour?" she asked.

"Actually, you caught me just as I was about to hit the shower," he told her. "So you can wait fifteen minutes or poke around on your own."

"I'll wait," she said. "Unless this is a bad time, in which case I can just go. I should have called first, anyway."

He waved off her apology. "You're always welcome. But I really need to clean up."

"Another hot date tonight?" she teased.

"Yeah," he said dryly. "With my brothers at Maxie's."

"Maxie's?" She wrinkled her nose. "Aren't you guys getting a little old for that scene?"

"We're guys," he reminded her, though he didn't disagree with her statement. "Our maturity level always lags behind our physical age."

"Tell me something I don't know."

He didn't have to think long to fulfill her request. "Luke has eight puppies he's trying to place in good homes."

Kelsey groaned. "Remind your brother that, in the past five years, he's already conned me into taking two cats, a parrot and an iguana."

"And you love the whole menagerie."

"That doesn't mean I'm taking any more," she said firmly.

"Brittney's always wanted a puppy," he pointed out.

"Unfortunately, the residences at Northeastern have a strictly enforced 'no pets' policy, so she'll have to be satisfied with visiting yours when she comes home."

He shook his head. "I'm not taking one of Luke's puppies." He tried to sound firm—to ignore the voice in the back of his head that promised the twins would be absolutely overjoyed if he did. And when the twins were happy, Georgia was happy, and her smile did all kinds of crazy things to his insides.

"You were going to shower," Kelsey reminded him.

He nodded and turned away. He did need to wash away all of the sawdust and sweat—and he was hopeful that the chilly spray might finally help banish wayward thoughts of Georgia that continued to pop into his mind.

Georgia didn't let herself think twice. If she did, she would think of all kinds of reasons that walking across the yard and knocking on Matt's door was a bad idea. Then she'd convince herself not to do it and she'd end up eating two dozen freshly baked chocolate chip cookies all by herself. Besides, it was just a plate of cookies—it wasn't as if she was propositioning her neighbor. Even if there was something about the man that intrigued her, despite the fact that she didn't want to be intrigued.

He was more attractive than any man had a right to be, but it wasn't just his physical appearance that appealed to her. There was a warmth in his eyes that hinted at a kindness in his soul, and a twinkle in his smile that attested to a sense of humor. And when he looked at her, she felt some of the weariness in her bones fade away and an unexpected warmth spread through her belly. Which was just one more reason she should not be making the man cookies.

She'd meant what she'd said to Jack the night before—she wasn't interested in any kind of romantic relationship and she didn't want to send mixed signals. On the other hand, it was possible that Jack had misinterpreted his brother's intentions and that Matt wasn't even reading any of her signals. Just because the man gave *her* tingles didn't mean that *he* felt the same sizzle of attraction. After all, it was extremely unlikely the sexy doctor would ever be interested in a weary widow with a lot of kid-sized baggage.

The mental lecture didn't do much to reassure her, but she accepted that the truth needed to be faced. Her children were her priority right now, and it would be a very long time before she even considered adding a man into the equation. So resolved, she lifted a hand to press the buzzer.

A moment later, she heard light footsteps—much lighter than she would have expected from a man of her neighbor's size and build—then the door was opened.

"Oh. Um." Georgia wasn't expecting anyone but Matt to answer the door, and finding herself face-to-face with a stunningly beautiful brunette left her momentarily speechless.

"You're looking for Matt," the woman guessed.

"I was," Georgia admitted. "But I don't want to interrupt—"

"Please." The other woman laughed as she held up a hand to halt her apology. "You're not interrupting anything."

"Are you sure?"

"Matt is a very old and close friend and nothing more than a friend. I just stopped by to drop off a housewarming gift and to make sure he was getting settled," she explained, stepping away from the door so Georgia could enter.

She held out the plate of cookies. "Actually, if I could just leave these with—"

"Georgia."

Before she could make her escape, he was there—fresh out of the shower, if his damp hair and the subtle scent of soap were any indication. And when he smiled at her, a smile filled with both warmth and pleasure, her heart actually skipped a beat.

"I'm sorry for just stopping by. I didn't know you had company."

"Kelsey's not company," Matt said, winking at the brunette.

The other woman rolled her eyes. "Didn't I tell you?"

Georgia smiled, then turned to offer the plate to Matt. "When you fixed up Shane's arm, you mentioned that you were partial to chocolate chip."

"I am," he agreed. "But I'm not sure I follow the connection between the hospital and the baked goods."

"I wanted to thank you for last night," she said, then felt her cheeks heat. She glanced at Kelsey and hastened to explain. "For dinner, I mean." And then, to clarify further, "When I lived in Manhattan, I didn't socialize with the people in my building—to be honest, I didn't even know most of them—so this whole neighbor-helping-neighbor thing is all new to me. But you've been really great, and I thought baking some cookies might be a nice way to say thanks."

"It wasn't necessary, but I appreciate it." He breathed in deeply. "They smell fantastic."

"Well, I should get back," she said.

"How is Shane managing with the cast?" Kelsey asked.

Georgia must have looked startled by the question, because the other woman smiled.

"Brittney, your hospital assistant and babysitter, is my daughter," she explained.

"Your daughter?" Georgia was genuinely baffled by this revelation. "You don't look old enough to be the mother of a seventeen-year-old."

Kelsey laughed. "Oh, I *do* like you."

"Shane's doing okay," she said, in response to the original question. "Mostly because his brother is catering to his every whim. Although I suspect that will wear thin in another day or two."

"How's Pippa?" Matt asked. "Has she been sleeping any better?"

She shook her head again.

"Colic doesn't last forever," he told her.

"It only seems like forever," Kelsey warned.

"It already does," Georgia admitted.

"And yet," Kelsey mused thoughtfully, "somehow a woman who has her hands full with three small children, including a fussy newborn and a preschooler with a broken arm, still found the time to make cookies for her new neighbor."

"It took a lot less time to make the cookies than it would have to cut my grass, which Matt did for me the other day," Georgia explained, wanting to ensure that Kelsey didn't get any wrong ideas.

"So this is…tit for tat?"

Georgia wasn't sure if the emphasis on "tit" and "tat" was

deliberate, but the implication had her cheeks flooding with color again. “Something like that,” she agreed lightly.

“Did you want some of these cookies and a cup of coffee? I could make decaf,” Matt said, coming to her rescue again.

“Thanks, but I just had a cup of tea with Mrs. Dunford—and I’ve left her alone with the kids for too long already.” She turned back to Kelsey. “It was nice meeting you.”

“You, too,” Kelsey said. “Next time, I hope you’ll have time for that cup of coffee.”

“That would be nice,” Georgia said.

Matt followed her to the door. “Sorry about Kelsey.”

Her lips curved. “Why are you sorry?”

“Because she’s the sister I never wanted.”

Despite the disclaimer, the tolerant affection she’d seen when Matt looked at Kelsey had been obvious. But when she glanced up now to find him looking at her, what she saw in his eyes wasn’t tolerant affection but something hotter and more intense. And this time, the tingles that started low in her belly spread through her whole body.

She had to swallow before she could speak. “I really have to get back.”

“Thanks again for the cookies.”

“Thank you,” she said. “For everything.”

He smiled. “See? You’re getting the hang of small-town living.”

“I’m trying,” she agreed.

“And from the neighbor-helping-neighbor thing, it’s just a short hop, skip and a jump to friendship.”

“I haven’t had a chance to meet many new people since I moved here,” she admitted. “I’d like it if we could be friends.”

“I’d like that, too,” he said.

Matt stayed where he was, watching until Georgia had disappeared through the back door and into her house.

In the few weeks since he’d moved in, he’d made more

progress with the beautiful blonde next door than he'd anticipated. She'd gone from being distant and wary to baking cookies for him, which gave him confidence that they were well on their way to becoming friends.

And from there, he was optimistic that it was just another hop, skip and a jump to something more.

Chapter Six

Matt stayed out with Luke and Jack later than he'd intended. Not because he was having a good time, but he figured if he at least pretended he was, it might get his brothers off his back for a while. He had a couple of beers early in the evening, because Luke was buying, but then he switched to soda. It was rare for Matt to overindulge, he never had more than a couple of drinks when he was driving, and he didn't drink at all if he was on call.

By the time he left the bar, his head was pounding from the throbbing beat of the music, his muscles ached from the sawing and hammering he'd done in the afternoon, and he was exhausted. And when he pulled into his driveway at nearly 2:00 a.m., he was stunned to see Georgia carrying Pippa's car seat toward her own vehicle, with the twins—in their pajamas—shuffling along beside her.

He shifted into Park and turned off his vehicle. Even through the closed window of his car, he could hear the baby's cries. In fact, he wouldn't be surprised if she was screaming loud enough to wake Mrs. Dunford across the street—and she was almost 80 percent deaf.

As he exited the vehicle, he had to admire the baby's lung capacity. He lifted a hand in greeting, but Georgia didn't see him. And as she passed beneath the streetlight, he saw that Pippa wasn't the only who was crying. The wet streaks on Georgia's cheeks were his undoing. He forgot his own fatigue and crossed the patch of grass that separated their two driveways.

"What are you doing?"

She finished locking the car seat into its base, then made sure the boys were securely belted in their booster seats. Straightening, she wiped the telltale traces of tears from her cheeks. "I'm going for a drive."

"At 2:00 a.m.?"

"Is that a violation of street curfew?"

"No, just common sense," he told her.

She reached for the driver's-side door, but he scooped the keys out of her hand.

"What are *you* doing?" she demanded.

"You're too exhausted and emotional to get behind the wheel of a car," he said. "Especially with your infant daughter and two little boys in the backseat."

"I'm tired because Pippa won't sleep. Hopefully, a quick trip around the block will change that, then I can come back home and we'll all get some shut-eye."

He opened the passenger-side door and gestured for her to get inside. She just stared at him, uncomprehending.

"I'll drive," he told her.

She opened her mouth as if to protest, then closed it again without saying a word and climbed into the vehicle.

He knew she wasn't accustomed to having anyone look out for her, and that she was probably more suspicious than appreciative of his efforts, but tonight she was too tired to put up a fight.

He'd just turned onto Queen Street when he realized that she was right—the motion of the car had quickly succeeded in putting Pippa to sleep. A glance in the rearview mirror confirmed that both Quinn's and Shane's eyes were closed, too. He started to comment to Georgia on the obvious success of her plan, then saw that she was as deeply asleep as her children.

Matt continued to drive, with only the radio for company, because he was concerned that Georgia would wake up as soon as he pulled back into her driveway, and he knew that she needed the rest as much as—or maybe even more than—her daughter. But half an hour later, his eyes were starting to feel heavy, too, so he turned the vehicle back toward Larkspur Drive.

Luckily, Georgia's house key was on the same ring as the van key, so he was able to let her sleep while he opened up the door and transferred the kids, one at a time, from the vehicle to their beds. He couldn't figure out how to unlatch Pippa's car seat, so he finally just unbuckled the belt and lifted the sleeping baby into his arms. She didn't stir. Obviously her sleepless nights were taking as much of a toll on the baby as they were on her mother.

When Pippa was settled in her crib, he went out to the van again to rouse Georgia. He touched her shoulder gently; she jolted.

"What— Where?"

"You're home," he told her.

She turned automatically to the backseat. "Where are the kids?"

"They're all inside, tucked into their beds."

Her eyes widened. "Really?"

He nodded. "Now it's your turn."

"Okay." She let him help her out of the car and toward the back door. "I didn't mean to fall asleep, too."

"Obviously you needed it."

"I guess so," she said, and lifted a hand to cover her yawn.

He steered her in the direction of the staircase. She automatically turned toward Pippa's room, but he guided her across the hall to what he assumed was her own. "Just go to sleep," he said softly.

"Pippa—"

"Is already in her crib."

"I should change her diaper."

"I checked it before I put her down."

She blinked. "You did?"

He smiled. "She's clean and dry and sleeping—you should do the same."

"Okay," she finally relented. Then she lay down on top of the covers, fully dressed, and closed her eyes.

"Sweet dreams, Georgia."

But she didn't respond, because she was dead to the world again.

Georgia awoke in a panic.

The sun was streaming through the partially open blinds and a quick glance at the clock on her bedside table revealed that it was 8:02 a.m.

She didn't believe it. The last time she'd nursed Pippa was around two, just before she'd gone out to the car to take her for a drive. But Pippa had never slept for six straight hours. She wondered if she might have awakened in the night and nursed the baby without realizing it, but her painfully engorged breasts immediately refuted the possibility.

Aside from the uncomfortable fullness, she felt good. Relaxed and rejuvenated. She crossed the hall to Pippa's room, a genuinely contented smile on her face.

The contentment and the smile disappeared fast when she discovered that her little girl's crib was empty.

She bolted across the hall to the twins' room and found it

was empty, too. She raced for the stairs, her heart hammering against her ribs. "Pippa?"

She couldn't have said why she was calling for her—she knew the baby wouldn't answer. But she wasn't thinking rationally. She wasn't thinking about anything except that her children weren't where they were supposed to be.

"She's here." Matt must have heard the panic in her voice, because he met her at the bottom of the stairs with Pippa in his arms and Quinn and Shane at his side.

Her breath rushed out of her lungs and her knees went weak. Matt reached out, catching her arm to hold her steady. "You okay?"

She nodded as she took Pippa, cuddling the little girl close to her chest. The baby cooed happily. "I am now."

"Why is Mommy crying?" Shane wanted to know.

She hadn't known that she was, and wiped hastily at her cheeks with her free hand, then touched his head. "I just got scared when I woke up and didn't know where you guys were."

"Pippa's a Who-dee-na, too," Quinn announced.

"Houdini," Matt corrected the boy automatically. Then, to Georgia, "I'm sorry. I thought I was doing you a favor by letting you get some sleep."

"You were. You did. I just didn't expect that you'd still be here, and when I saw that her crib was empty and I didn't hear the boys…" They wandered off now, back into the living room where she could hear their favorite cartoons on the television.

"You panicked. Understandably," he said. "And I'm sorry."

She wanted to be mad, but he was so genuinely contrite that she couldn't hold on to her anger. Especially not when he spoke again and asked, "Are you hungry? I hope you don't mind but I pilfered through your cupboards and was just about to make some French toast."

"No, I don't mind," she said. "Especially not if you're offering to make French toast for me, too."

"Absolutely," he assured her. "If for no other reason than to be able to tell my brothers that I had breakfast with my beautiful new neighbor."

She knew he was teasing, and she wasn't sure how she was supposed to respond to that. From their first meeting, he'd been friendly and flirtatious, but maybe he was just the type of guy who flirted with every woman who crossed his path. Because the idea that he could be interested continued to baffle her—and never more so than right now, as she suddenly remembered her wrinkled clothing, disheveled hair and unbrushed teeth.

"Do I have time for a quick shower?" she asked.

"Twenty minutes enough?"

She nodded and turned back toward the stairs.

"Are you planning to take Pippa into the shower with you?"

"No, but I figured she was overdue for a feeding," she said. Despite the fact that the baby certainly wasn't acting like it had been more than six hours since her last feeding, Georgia's aching breasts confirmed the fact.

"She had a bottle an hour ago," he said.

That stopped her abruptly in her tracks. "She had a bottle?"

"I found your stash of breast milk in the freezer."

Georgia was impressed, and more than a little surprised. Because on the few occasions that she'd tried to coax her daughter to take one, Pippa had refused to latch on to the artificial nipple. "She was okay with the bottle?"

"She was hungry," he said simply.

She couldn't help but smile as she secured Pippa into her bouncy chair. "You really do go above and beyond, don't you?"

"It wasn't a big deal," he assured her.

But to Georgia it was. Six hours of uninterrupted sleep was a very big deal—and she was very grateful. But now she wondered, "Where did *you* sleep?"

"Your couch, in the living room."

Having caught some quick naps there herself, she didn't recommend it. "I hope you don't have to work today," she said, wondering how he could get through a day at the hospital on only a few hours of sleep on a sofa.

"I work twelve-hour shifts for four days, then I'm off for four days, barring emergencies. This is one of my days off."

"Then you should be taking advantage of the opportunity to laze around in bed."

His lips curved. "Is that an invitation?"

"No!" She was shocked by the idea—and just a little bit tempted by the wickedly explicit thoughts that sprang to mind in response to his suggestion. "I only meant that you didn't have to hang around here taking care of my kids."

"I like your kids," he told her.

And they absolutely adored Matt, but that was hardly the point. She couldn't help but remember what Jack had said about his brother and worry that she was taking advantage of his generous nature. She hadn't asked him to help her out last night, but she hadn't objected to his offer, either. And she certainly hadn't asked him to spend the night so that she could get some sleep, but she was immensely grateful that he'd done so.

Matt took a step closer, lifted a hand to tuck an errant strand of hair behind her ear. "And I like you."

The contact was brief, casual. But the touch made her shiver; her heart started to pound; her throat went dry.

All he'd done was touch her, and her hormones had gone haywire. Was she so lonely, so desperate for human contact, that such a simple gesture could affect her so deeply? Apparently so, because not only was her pulse racing, her body was aching, yearning.

"Well, I'm going to go take that shower now," she said, and turned to make her escape.

What was he doing?

It was a question Matt had asked himself countless times

through the night and one that continued to plague his mind as he got breakfast under way.

He found a package of bacon in the fridge, started the meat frying on the stove while he gathered the rest of the tools and ingredients for French toast. The twins had been playing in the living room but, drawn by the sounds emanating from the kitchen, ventured into the room to investigate.

Quinn looked quizzical as he watched Matt turn the strips of bacon that were sizzling and popping. "Are you really gonna make breakfast?"

"Sure." He set a lid over the bacon to cut down on the grease spatters.

"Can I watch?"

"Sure," he said again. "You can even help, if you want."

The little boy's eyes went wide. "Really?"

"Why not?"

Shane, silent until now, frowned. "Daddies don't cook."

"Says who?" Matt challenged.

"My daddy."

The assertion, so firmly stated, gave Matt pause. He didn't want to contradict any memories the boys had of their father, but he couldn't imagine that Georgia wanted her sons growing up with the outdated assumption that the kitchen was strictly a woman's domain. "Your dad never scrambled eggs for you on a Sunday morning so your mom could sleep in?"

Shane shook his head. "Mommy doesn't sleep in."

Which was apparently a situation that had existed long before Pippa came along.

"She slept in today," Quinn pointed out.

"And we're going to make her breakfast today," Matt said.

"We could order pizza."

Matt had to smile. "For breakfast?"

"Daddy knew the best places to get pizza," Quinn said loyally.

"Well, I'm going to make French toast. And if you don't want to help, I'll crack all the eggs myself."

Shane shifted closer, looked up at him with solemn dark eyes. "I wanna crack eggs."

"Then let's get you washed up," Matt said.

He supervised the boys' washing their hands, or—in Shane's case—washing the only hand he would be using. Then he sat them at the table with a big bowl and gave them each three eggs while he took the bacon out of the frying pan and set it on paper towels to absorb the grease.

"Hey! You're not 'sposed to put the shell in the bowl."

Matt glanced over in time to see that Quinn's criticism had Shane's eyes filling with tears.

"It's hard with one hand," Shane said, his voice wavering.

"You're doing a great job," he assured the child. "And it's easy enough to fish the pieces of shell out again," he told Quinn. Then he gave Shane a spoon and showed him how to do it.

But Quinn was still scowling over his brother's clumsiness. "What if he doesn't get them all?"

"Then we'll have an extra dose of calcium with our breakfast."

"What's calsum?" Shane asked.

"It helps build strong bones and teeth."

"Like milk," Quinn said.

"That's right," Matt agreed. "Because milk is a source of calcium."

He poured a generous splash of it into the bowl with the eggs and let them take turns whisking the mixture. After reminding them that they should never go near the stove without an adult close by to supervise, he let them each dip a piece of bread in the liquid and then place it in the frying pan.

It was as much fun for Matt as it obviously was for the twins, and all the while, that same question echoed in the back of his mind: What was he doing?

But this time, the answer was obvious: He was getting too close.

Aside from the fact that she was a widow, he knew very few details about Georgia's life before she came to Pinehurst. Had her marriage been a happy one? Was she still in love with and mourning her husband? What did she want for her future?

Of course, he didn't know the answers to any of those questions. He only knew that he was extremely attracted to her—and totally captivated by her children. They were a family without a daddy, and he very much wanted to be a daddy again.

That, he knew, was his problem. He wasn't sure that he could separate his desire for Georgia from his affection for her children. And the closer he got to all of them, the more difficult it would be. He needed to take a step back, distance himself from the situation.

So that was what he was going to do—right after breakfast.

Chapter Seven

Georgia did feel better after her shower. Fresh and well-rested, and completely in control of her wayward hormones. She could smell bacon and coffee as she made her way down the stairs and inhaled deeply, confirming that Matt had found the tin of French roast her mother kept in the freezer. Georgia had given up caffeine when she found out she was pregnant with Pippa and, more than a year later, it was the one thing she still craved. Unfortunately, Pippa's fussiness and sleeplessness ensured that it was something she continued to avoid.

"Mommy's coming!" She heard Quinn's excited whisper summoning his brother.

Shane appeared at the bottom of the stairs. He was still in his pajamas, but he bent at the waist in an awkward bow. "I'm your eksort."

"And a very handsome escort you are," she told him, and was rewarded with one of his shy smiles.

She took his hand and let him lead her to the dining room where the table had been set with mismatched plates on Mickey Mouse place mats with a centerpiece of wilting dandelions in a drinking glass. Georgia took in the scene in about two seconds, and that quickly, the firm grip she held on her emotions slipped.

During their eight-year marriage, Phillip had taken her to plenty of fancy restaurants with exclusive menus and exemplary service. But no Crepes Suzette or Eggs Benedict had ever looked as appealing to Georgia as the platter of overcooked bacon and slightly mangled French toast on her mother's dining room table.

She swallowed around the lump in her throat. "Somebody's been busy."

"We were!" Quinn said proudly. "We made it together—all of us."

She didn't—couldn't—look at Matt, because she didn't want him to see the tears that swam in her eyes. Instead, she focused on her boys. "Did you really?"

"'Cept for Pippa," Shane told her.

Georgia noticed that Matt had moved the baby's bouncy chair into the dining room so that her mother would be able to keep an eye on her while she had breakfast. Pippa kicked her legs and smiled now, as if she knew that she was the subject of their conversation.

"You did a wonderful job," Georgia said, and because Matt had spearheaded the effort, she lifted her gaze to meet his now. "Thank you."

"You're welcome." He pulled out a chair for her. "Now sit and eat before it gets cold."

The brusque command was exactly what she needed to keep the tears at bay. Following his direction, she sat and loaded up her plate. But before she could sample her own breakfast, she had to cut Shane's French toast. Then she turned to do the same for Quinn, only to find that Matt had already completed the task.

"Eat," he said again, though more gently this time.

So she sliced off a corner of the fried bread and popped it into her mouth.

"Do you like it, Mommy?" She heard the anxiousness in Shane's voice and wondered why it was that her youngest son worried so much about doing everything just right while his sibling always forged ahead without concern. Sometimes it was hard to believe they were brothers, never mind twins.

"It is the best French toast I have ever tasted," she assured him.

"That's 'cuz it's got extra calsum," Quinn told her. "From the shells Shane dropped in the bowl."

She sent a quizzical glance in Matt's direction. He just smiled and lifted one shoulder.

"That must be it," she agreed.

Georgia ate two slices of French toast and three strips of bacon and savored every bite. When the twins had finished their breakfast, they carried their plates and cups to the kitchen and went to wash up.

As she heard them clamoring up the stairs, she turned to Matt. "Thank you," she said again. "Not just for cooking breakfast, but for including the boys in the process."

"It was fun." He said it so simply and matter-of-factly, she knew he meant it.

"Can I ask you something?"

"Sure."

"Why aren't you married?"

The blunt question seemed to take him aback, and he lifted his mug for a sip of coffee before answering. "I was," he finally admitted. "Now I'm divorced."

She winced. "Excuse me while I take my foot out of my mouth."

"No need. The divorce was final more than three years ago. I'm over it. Mostly."

"Mostly?"

He shrugged. "It's always hard to accept the loss of something you really wanted."

A truth that she knew far too well. And though she knew it was a question she had no right to ask and none of her business anyway, she heard herself say, "Do you still love her?"

"No." This time he replied without hesitation and emphasized the response with a shake of his head. "Whatever feelings we'd once had for one another were gone long before the divorce papers were signed."

"Then why aren't you dating anyone?"

"How do you know I'm not?" he challenged.

"Because you spent Saturday night sleeping on my couch."

He smiled at that. "Okay, I'm not."

"Why not?" she asked again.

"I've been out with a few people—I just haven't met anyone who made me want to take the step from a few casual dates to a relationship."

"You're so great with my kids," she told him, "I'd have thought you had half a dozen of your own."

He looked away as he shook his head. "I don't."

And then, in an obvious effort to put an end to that topic of conversation, he reached across the table to tickle Pippa's bare toes. The baby kicked her legs and cooed joyfully in response to his attention.

"When she's happy, she's really happy, isn't she?"

Georgia smiled at her daughter. "Yeah. So much that I sometimes almost forget the hell she's been putting me through over the past few weeks."

He went to the kitchen to refill his mug of coffee, then returned to his seat across from her. "When did you say your mother would be back from Vegas?"

"The original plan was for her to come home yesterday."

"What happened?"

"She decided to go from Nevada to Montana."

He sipped his coffee. "Why Montana?"

"Because that's where her new husband lives."

His brows lifted. "When did she get married?"

"A few days ago."

"You don't approve of the man she married?" he guessed.

"I don't know him," she admitted. "In fact, *she* didn't know him before their eyes met across the baccarat table."

His lips curved. "She's a romantic."

"That's a more favorable word than the one I would have chosen," she admitted.

"I take it you're not a romantic?"

"I like to think I'm a little more...practical." It was so easy to open up to him, to tell him things she hadn't spoken aloud to anyone else—not even either of her sisters. In fact, if not for the way her body hummed whenever he was near, she might have thought that they could be friends.

But the awareness between them was too powerful for her to be completely comfortable in his presence. And when she glanced up to see him studying her, she was suddenly conscious that the awareness was sizzling even now.

"You've never been swept off your feet?" he challenged.

She shook her head. "I don't want a man to sweep me off my feet, although I wouldn't object to a man who was willing to sweep the floors every once in a while."

"I can sweep floors," he told her. "But I don't do windows."

She smiled. "I'll keep that in mind."

"No, you won't."

His blunt contradiction took her aback. "Excuse me?"

"You're so busy trying to do everything yourself that it doesn't occur to you to ask for help every once in a while."

"Maybe," she acknowledged. "But I'm learning to accept it when it's offered."

"That's a start," he said, and rose from the table to begin clearing the rest of the dishes.

Georgia gathered the napkins and cutlery and followed him into the kitchen.

"I don't like to feel inadequate," she finally admitted.

He turned and stared at her. "Are you kidding? You're juggling the responsibilities of a home, a job and raising three kids."

"Which is no more than a lot of women do."

"A lot of women have a partner to share the burden," he pointed out.

She dropped the napkins into the garbage and put the cutlery into the basket in the dishwasher. "Truthfully, even before Phillip died, he wasn't at home enough to share much of the burden." Then, because she didn't want to sound critical of the man she'd married, she felt compelled to add, "He was a good husband and father, but he had an incredibly demanding job. He worked a lot of long hours and weekends."

Too late, she recognized that she was making excuses about her husband to a man whose job as an orthopedic surgeon was undoubtedly more demanding and stressful than that of a trader. And yet, Matt didn't seem to have too much trouble making time for the things he enjoyed. Which was one of the concerns that had plagued her throughout her marriage: If Phillip really wanted to be with her, why had he chosen to spend so much time away from her?

She knew the situation wasn't that black-and-white, that her husband's drive originated from the hard lessons he'd learned in his life. And no matter what she said or did, she couldn't convince him that they should take time to enjoy what they had. It was never enough for Phillip—he wanted to work harder, earn more, buy more. In the end, he worked himself into an early grave, leaving his wife alone and his children without a father.

Her eyes filled again. Obviously she wasn't as in control of her emotions as she'd hoped, but this time she managed to hold the tears in check. "I'm sorry. I'm not usually such an emotional basket case."

"You don't have to apologize to me," he told her.

"Yes, I do. You've been nothing but helpful and kind, and I shouldn't repay you by crying on your shoulder."

"I'm not afraid of a few tears," he promised.

She managed a smile. "You're a good man, Matt Garrett."

"Don't say that too loud," he warned. "I have a reputation to protect."

"Believe me, every time I go into town I hear all about the string of broken hearts you left behind you in high school," she admitted. "Although rumor has it, you've matured into a responsible citizen since then."

"Just a nasty rumor," he assured her. "Don't believe it for a second."

This time, her smile came more easily.

However, before Georgia could respond, Shane ventured into the kitchen. "I builded a hosp'al with my bricks," he told her.

Since his trip to the E.R. the previous week, he'd been understandably curious about hospitals and doctors and everything related to the medical profession, so his chosen project was hardly a surprise to Georgia.

"Did you want me to come take a look at it?" she asked.

He nodded, then glanced shyly at Matt and quickly away again. "Dr. Matt, too."

"I'd love to take a look at it," Matt said.

And when he held out his hand to the little boy, Shane hesitated less than half a second before he lifted his own and tucked it inside the doctor's much larger one.

Georgia stood rooted to the spot as fresh tears pricked her eyes. Shane was her introverted son—the little boy who hovered in the background while his brother basked in the spotlight. It was rare for Shane to make any kind of overture, especially to a stranger.

Okay, so Matt wasn't exactly a stranger, but being neighbors for a few weeks didn't make him a close acquaintance, either. Of course, the fact that he'd fixed up the little boy's broken arm might have helped the doctor breach Shane's usual guard, but Georgia suspected her son's ready acceptance of the man had more to do with the man himself. And that was something she was going to have to think about.

When she entered the living room, she saw that Matt was already hunkered down beside the twins to examine their construction projects. He admired the "fine craftsmanship" of Shane's hospital and the "creative design" of Quinn's fire station and commented that there were enough bricks left over to build a whole city.

"Do you want to help us?" Quinn asked.

But Shane was shaking his head before Matt even had a chance to respond.

"Daddies don't play," he reminded his brother, and the matter-of-fact tone of his voice made Georgia's heart ache.

Phillip had loved his children—she had never ever doubted that fact. But she'd never understood, until she'd seen how easily Matt interacted with the boys, how much the twins had missed out on by not having a hands-on dad. She knew they'd felt rebuffed when Phillip had been too tired to show much interest in whatever they were doing, and she'd tried to make it up to them. But no matter what she did, she couldn't be the father they needed.

"Some adults don't have time to play," Matt acknowledged. "But sometimes adults need to play—" he glanced up at Georgia and grinned "—just to prove they're still kids at heart."

"Are you a kid at heart?" Quinn wanted to know.

"Definitely," Matt said, and dug into the bin of bricks to prove it.

Georgia left the boys to their toys and set about cleaning up the kitchen. Matt and the twins had made a pretty good attempt at destroying her mother's stove, but the wielding of a scrubber with some serious muscle eventually succeeding in removing the last traces of egg from the ceramic cooktop.

Still, the cleanup was a small price to pay for everything Matt had done for her. Not only had he let her sleep through the night—and oh, what a glorious indulgence that had been!—he'd helped her boys make breakfast for her. And now, when she thought he would have been more than anxious to get back to his own house and his own life, he was playing with her children, giving them the male attention they needed more desperately than she'd guessed.

But as grateful as she was to Matt, she was also wary. It was obvious to Georgia that the boys already adored their new neighbor and she was worried that they would start to rely on him for too much. Because as great as Matt had been, he wouldn't stick around. Because no man in her life had ever stuck around.

If that was cynical, well, she had reason to be cynical. Her biological father had walked out before she was three years old, and not one of the three stepfathers who had passed through her life had stayed for much longer than that. The few casual and short-lived relationships she'd had as a teenager had done nothing to alter her opinion. It wasn't until she met Phillip that she let herself look to the future and trust that he would be there. But it turned out that she'd been wrong about that.

She knew that her husband hadn't chosen to leave her, and yet, the end result was the same. He was gone and she was alone. Well, not entirely alone. And she would forever be grateful to Phillip for their three beautiful children.

But as happy as they seemed most of the time—discounting Pippa's colic for the moment—she couldn't help worrying about them, about the void in their lives that only a father could fill.

Since Phillip's death, she'd sometimes found herself wondering if Charlotte's string of impetuous unions had been—even in part—an attempt to provide her daughters with a sense of family. Except that her daughters were all grown up now and Charlotte was still following her heart—wherever it might lead.

Georgia had no intention of following that same path, not for any reason and certainly not on the hunt for a substitute father for her children. She wasn't willing to risk her heart again, and she certainly wasn't going to risk theirs.

But as she heard the boys giggling in response to something Matt had said or done in the other room, she had to wonder if it wasn't already too late.

Matt made a conscious effort to keep his distance from his neighbor and her kids over the next week. Work at the hospital kept him busy enough for the first few days—it was his days off that caused him trouble.

In the space of a few weeks, he'd become accustomed to seeing Georgia and her kids almost every day, even if it was only for a few minutes of conversation on the sidewalk. He missed Quinn's endless barrage of questions, Shane's intense focus as he listened to his responses, and the joyful light in Pippa's eyes whenever she saw him. But mostly he missed spending time with Georgia.

Every time he pulled into his driveway, his gaze automatically swung toward the house next door. More than once, he considered stopping by just to see how she was doing and to check if the shadows under her eyes had faded. Too many times, he'd started to head in that direction before his self-preservation instincts kicked in and turned him around again.

Instead, he did some more work in the basement. He hung drywall, taped seams, plastered nail holes. The physical labor kept his hands busy, but it didn't stop him from thinking about Georgia. He spent some time hanging out with his brothers and took a fair bit of ribbing for having struck out with the beautiful blonde next door. It was easier to accept their jabs than admit that he'd walked away from the plate before the first pitch had ever been thrown. He'd been nicknamed Mr.

Clutch in high school, because he'd always played his best in the biggest games. But if this was a game, it was the big leagues, and there was more at stake here than a score.

Georgia wasn't just a beautiful woman, she was the mother of three beautiful children, and they were a package deal. He couldn't take one without the other, and he was afraid to admit how much he wanted the whole package. And so, instead of stepping up to the plate, he'd walked away. Mr. Clutch had been face-to-face with what was potentially the biggest opportunity in his life, and he'd choked. And if his brothers knew the truth, he'd never hear the end of it.

So he let them think that he'd struck out and he tried not to think about Georgia while he listened to Jack boast about the clerk who had propositioned him in the judge's chambers. But when Luke started rambling on about the exploits of the puppies, he couldn't help but remember how totally enthralled the twins had been by them—and that those puppies had played a pivotal role in his first meeting with his neighbors.

It was readily apparent that Luke was trying to convince one or both of his brothers that their lives would not be complete without a canine companion. He'd found good homes for five of them, he admitted, and had decided to keep one for himself, which meant that there were only two left.

Jack, who was hardly ever at the penthouse apartment he paid an astronomical rent for, refused to be swayed. He didn't have the time or the energy that a puppy would demand, not to mention the havoc that an untrained animal would wreak on his designer furniture and hardwood floors.

So Luke gave up on Jack and focused his efforts on his other brother. Matt was able to tune out most of his arguments, but he couldn't forget the awe and excitement on both Quinn's and Shane's faces when they'd seen the puppies in his backyard. And he couldn't forget the stubbornness and longing in Shane's voice when he told his mother, "We *do* want a puppy."

And Matt knew he was fighting a losing battle, because he couldn't refuse anything that would put a smile on the boys' faces—and maybe Georgia's, too.

Chapter Eight

Matt was avoiding her.

Georgia didn't know why, but she knew it was true.

There was a part of her that insisted the "why" didn't matter. All that mattered was that Matt had done what she expected him to do—he'd walked away. But another part insisted that there had to be a reason for his withdrawal. And whether or not he wanted to be friends, they were neighbors, and she didn't want there to be any awkwardness between them when their paths crossed.

More than a week after he'd made her breakfast, on a rare night in which Pippa had actually settled down at a reasonable hour, she waited outside on her back porch to catch him when he came home from work.

She recognized the quiet hum of the engine as he pulled into his driveway, and her heart started to beat just a little bit faster.

She was unaccountably nervous, and already second-guessing her decision to confront him. Maybe he hadn't been avoiding her. Maybe he'd just been busy. Or—and this was a possibility that left her slightly unsettled—maybe he'd done some thinking after their breakfast conversation and had started dating someone. And wouldn't she feel like a complete idiot if she went over there now and he wasn't alone?

She decided that knocking on his door after ten o'clock at night, in the absence of an emergency, might make it look like she'd been waiting for him. And although she had been, she didn't want him to know it. A realization that only made her feel more ridiculous.

She had just turned to go back into the house when the light over Matt's deck came on and he stepped outside. Alone.

He dropped down onto the top step, his forearms on his knees, a beer bottle dangling from his fingertips.

Georgia hesitated. She was pretty good at reading body language, and the weariness in Matt's broad shoulders was visible even in the shadows from fifty feet away. He lifted the bottle to his lips, took a long swallow.

Her decision made, she ducked back into the house to make sure all of the kids were settled and sleeping, then she clipped the baby monitor onto her belt and made her way across the yard.

Despite his preoccupation, he must have heard her footsteps rustling in the grass, because his head came up and he peered into the darkness. She stepped into the circle of light.

"Georgia." She saw surprise flit across his face and heard the pleasure in his voice before he seemed to shut down all of his emotions.

It confirmed her suspicion—he had been avoiding her. For some reason, he was deliberately trying to put distance between them. But right now, she didn't care about any of that. All that concerned her was the look of abject misery on his face.

"Rough day?"

He just nodded.

Though he hadn't invited her to sit down, she did so anyway, settling onto the step beside him. "Can I do anything?"

He shook his head and lifted the bottle to his lips again.

The silence stretched between them, broken only by the chirp of crickets and the occasional hoot of an owl in the distance.

"Want to talk about it?"

He shook his head again. "Not really."

She waited another minute, hoping he would change his mind. He remained silent, and she pushed herself back to her feet.

"But I wouldn't mind if you stayed awhile," he said. "I thought I wanted to be alone, but that's not really a great place right now."

She glanced back at her own house. It wasn't really so far, but she didn't like to be away from her children, even when they were sleeping. "Can you bring your beer over to my step?"

"You want to be able to hear the kids," he guessed.

"I know it seems silly when I have this—" she tapped the monitor clipped on her belt "—but I feel more comfortable being close."

"It doesn't seem silly at all," he told her, rising to his feet. "In fact, I wish more parents were as concerned about their children as you are."

She sensed that his comment was somehow connected to his dark mood, and wondered what had happened at the hospital. He'd already said he didn't want to talk about it, and she didn't want to pry, but she wanted him to know that she was there for him—as he'd been for her when she needed him.

When they were settled on her deck, she decided to open up the channels of communication. Even if they didn't talk about what was bothering him, she thought it might help him just to talk.

"After living in Manhattan for so long, it took me a while

to get used to the sights and sounds outside of the city. It seems so quiet here—" she smiled wryly "—at least it is when Pippa's not screaming. At first, it seemed *too* quiet. But now, I sit out on the porch sometimes just to listen to the crickets, and I feel a sense of peace that I've never known anywhere else."

"I used to take it for granted," he admitted. "Growing up around here, I didn't really know anything else. But the years I spent away at college gave me a new appreciation for this town."

"I never thought I wanted anything like this. But now that I'm here, I can't imagine a more perfect place to raise my kids. I want to watch them run around the backyard, chasing butterflies and playing tag. I want to hear them giggle when they jump into piles of leaves we've raked up together."

"You'll have lots of leaves," he assured her, looking around at the towering maples that lined the back of her property. "Probably more than you want to rake."

"Luckily, I have this wonderful neighbor who's been a very big help with a lot of my outdoor chores."

"It's not as if I enjoy cutting the grass—actually, I do enjoy cutting the grass," he decided, sounding almost surprised by the realization. "The mindless physical work is a welcome diversion after a twelve-hour shift at the hospital."

"Then I'm sure raking leaves in the fall will provide similar benefits."

"And shoveling snow?"

She smiled. "If it works for you, I wouldn't want to deprive you of the pleasure."

"Believe me, there are other—and much more pleasurable—stress releases."

She felt her cheeks color, but refused to follow where his train of thought was trying to lead her. "Talking about the cause of stress also helps," she agreed.

"I wasn't talking about talking," he informed her.

"I know," she admitted. "But it can help. And if you ever decide you do want to talk, I'm happy to listen."

He was silent for a moment, considering her offer. She didn't expect he would actually open up to her. It had been apparent that whatever was bothering him wasn't something he wanted to discuss, but he finally said, "I performed surgery on a four-year-old girl with a spiral fracture tonight."

"What's a spiral fracture?"

"It's a break caused by twisting the bone—a common type of injury suffered by skiers. Their feet are tied into boots locked into skis, and when a ski twists around, the leg automatically twists with it."

"It seems unlikely that she was skiing anywhere around here in May."

"She wasn't. And it wasn't her leg, it was her arm."

It didn't take her long to make the logical jump. "She was abused?"

"The mother is denying it, but X-rays revealed that the child's arm had been broken before and healed improperly because it wasn't treated. So when I fixed the new break, I also had to rebreak and repair the previous injury."

Georgia's eyes filled with tears. "And she's only four?"

He nodded.

"I'd say that was a pretty rough day," she agreed.

"I'm doing okay now."

She touched her lips to his. Softly. Briefly.

He stilled. "What was that for?"

"A kiss to make it better," she said lightly. "Because you're hurting."

Georgia started to draw back, but Matt snaked his arm around her waist and held her close.

"I'm feeling a lot of things right now," he told her. "And hurt isn't anywhere near the top of the list."

Her eyes grew wide, her breath hitched, and he could see the pulse point at the base of her jaw fluttering.

"I think we're getting a little sidetracked," she hedged.

"Are we? Or are we finally back on the track that we've been heading toward all along?"

"How is it possible that we were heading anywhere in the same direction when you've been avoiding me all week?"

His lips curved, just a little. "Did you miss me?"

"Yes," she admitted, sounding piqued. "For almost three weeks, it seemed as if I couldn't step outside my door without tripping over you, and then, just when I got used to you being around—when I started looking forward to you being around—you disappeared."

"If it counts for anything, I missed you, too. All of you."

Her gaze softened. "The boys kept asking me why you didn't want to play with them anymore."

"I'm sorry," he said, and meant it.

"I don't want you to be sorry, I just want to know if it was something I said or did."

"No," he assured her. "It's all on me."

"Why?"

"Because I knew that if I didn't put some space between us I wouldn't be able to stop myself from doing this."

She knew he was going to kiss her. He could see the conflict in her eyes—the war between wariness and wanting. Not wanting to give her another second to worry or wonder, he dipped his head.

She held herself immobile and kept her eyes open, as if she was willing to tolerate his efforts but was determined not to participate. He kept his gaze locked on hers, his hand splayed against her lower back, as he brushed his mouth against hers. A soft sigh sounded in her throat and her eyelids flickered, just a little, proving she wasn't as immune to him as she wanted to believe.

Since the end of his marriage, he'd been with other women,

but sex without intimacy had left him feeling oddly unfulfilled. The problem with meaningless flings, he'd quickly discovered, was that they were meaningless. Truthfully, Georgia was the first woman he'd been sincerely attracted to in a long time, the first woman with whom he could imagine himself having a relationship rather than a one-night stand.

He also realized that he was probably thinking further ahead than she was. She was a young widow with three kids, and he knew he would have to take things slow until he was sure she wanted the same thing he did. Right now, she didn't seem to know what she wanted—but at least he knew he had her full attention.

His mouth cruised over hers again, savoring her texture and flavor. Her lips were soft, lush and deliciously seductive. He traced the shape with the tip of his tongue, and swallowed her soft sigh as her eyelids finally drifted shut.

He took his time, teasing her lips further apart, testing her response. She lifted her hands to his chest, and he half expected her to push him away. He would have been disappointed, but not really surprised. But then her hands slid over his shoulders to link behind his head, and she pressed herself closer, so that her breasts were crushed against his chest, her hips pressed against his.

She had to know he was aroused—there was no way she could think the erection throbbing inside the front of his pants was anything else—but she didn't pull away. His hand slid under the hem of her T-shirt, skimmed up her back. She shivered in response to his touch on her bare skin and moaned in pleasure. It was that low, sexy sound deep in her throat—proof that she wanted this every bit as much as he did—that nearly undid him.

He'd wanted to kiss her—and now that he had, he wanted so much more. But he'd promised himself that he would take things slow, which was a lot harder to do than he'd expected with his heart pounding so fiercely inside his chest and his blood pulsing hotly in his veins.

He eased his lips from hers but kept his arms around her to ensure she couldn't flee. Because he could see, even in eyes still clouded with desire, the first hint of panic beginning to set in. And her words, when she spoke, confirmed her worry.

"That was a really bad idea," she told him.

"I have to disagree."

"We're neighbors and, hopefully, friends."

"I'd say that's a good start to any relationship."

She shook her head. "I'm not looking for a relationship."

"Because you're still grieving for your husband," he guessed.

"Because I need to focus on my kids," she clarified. "And they don't leave me enough time or energy for any kind of romantic involvement."

"Okay—we'll put a hold on the romance portion of things."

"That includes the kissing portion."

"You kissed me first," he pointed out.

"Not like that," she protested.

"You didn't like the way I kissed you?"

She rolled her eyes. "Is your ego so fragile that you need to fish for compliments?"

"So you *did* enjoy kissing me," he surmised.

"It seems you're a man of many talents, Dr. Garrett."

"That kiss barely scratched the surface."

"That's what I'm afraid of," she admitted.

"There's something between us," he told her.

"It's a basic physical attraction."

"It's more than that."

She shook her head again. "I won't let it be anything more than that."

He smiled. "You think it's your decision to make?"

"Yes." Her tone was firm and unequivocal. "I make my

own choices, and I'm *not* getting romantically involved with you."

But he caught the slightest hint of desperation in her tone now and was torn between wanting to offer reassurance and challenge her conviction. Instead, he opted for a casual shrug. "Okay."

Her gaze narrowed suspiciously. "Okay?"

"You've obviously made up your mind," he acknowledged.

"I have," she confirmed. "And I appreciate that you're respecting my decision."

"I do," he agreed. "But that doesn't mean I'm not going to do everything in my power to change your mind."

"You'll be wasting your time," she warned.

He shrugged again. "I figure it's my time to waste."

Her sigh was filled with exasperation. "But why would you want to waste your time with me when there are any number of women in this town who would be thrilled to be with you?"

He grinned. "Any number, huh?"

"As if you didn't know that everywhere you and your brothers go, female heads swivel in your direction."

"It's been like that since high school," he admitted. "It's a curse."

"And how long ago was high school?" she asked, in what seemed to him an abrupt shift in the conversation.

"Almost twenty years," he admitted. "Why?"

"Because in the past few weeks, every time I go into town someone refers to me as the young mother from New York City who moved in next to Dr. Garrett—conveniently overlooking the fact that I was here before you. And on top of that, I've had at least half a dozen people tell me about the grand slam home run you knocked out of the park in the bottom of the thirteenth inning to bring home the district championship."

"Only half a dozen?" He frowned. "I guess my legend is truly fading."

She just shook her head.

"Did you ever play baseball?" he asked.

"Just in gym class at school or the occasional pick-up game at the park when I was a kid."

"Are you any good?"

"I was never the first one picked for a team, but I wasn't the last, either."

"Because we play a co-ed charity softball tournament on the Fourth of July and I'm putting together a team, if you're interested."

She shook her head. "I'm not playing any games with you—you're completely out of my league."

"I got to first base with you tonight," he teased. "And you didn't seem to have any trouble keeping up."

Her cheeks flushed. "It won't happen again."

He just grinned. "I guess time will tell."

"Matt," she said warningly.

"I'll see you soon," he promised.

His step was much lighter as he made his way across the grass to his own house, and he knew the sizzling kiss he'd shared with Georgia was only part of the reason. Another—maybe even bigger part—was just being with her.

He hadn't appreciated how much he'd missed having someone to open up to at the end of a difficult day until she'd sat down beside him and invited him to talk. And she not only listened to him ramble about the stress of his day, she empathized with him. And then she'd kissed him.

True, it had been little more than a casual brush of her lips against his, but he figured it had to mean something that she'd made the first move.

He figured it meant even more that she hadn't balked—at least not too much—when he made the second.

A few days later, Matt had just walked into the house after a visit to his brother when his phone rang. Picking up the receiver, he was pleased to hear Georgia's voice on the other end of the line, and even more pleased when she said, "Have you had dinner yet?"

"No," he admitted.

"Because we just ordered a party tray of pizza and thought you might want to come over to share it with us."

"Why did you order a party tray?"

"Because it was the special of the day," she told him. "And because you've cooked for me—twice now—so it only seems fair for me to return the favor. I didn't actually make the pizza, but I thought I would earn some points by providing the meal."

"You're the only one keeping score," he said.

"Maybe, but the boys would like to share their pizza with you, if you don't have other plans."

Adding the kids to the equation obliterated any resistance. "I don't have other plans," he admitted. "And pizza sounds great, but would it be too much trouble if I asked you to bring it over here?"

"Not too much trouble," she told him, "but likely a lot of fingerprints you'll have to clean up around the house after."

"I'm not worried about fingerprints," he assured her.

"Then we'll be over in five."

As much as Georgia tried to convince herself that taking pizza over to Matt's house was just being neighborly, she knew that wasn't entirely true. One kiss had changed everything.

One unbelievably hot, mind-numbing, toe-curling kiss.

Since Matt had planted his lips on hers, all kinds of lustful thoughts had taken root in her mind. Thankfully, she wasn't just taking pizza but three kids, too, and she was grateful for the buffer that their presence would provide.

Maybe her hormones had been stirred up by that kiss, but she was confident that she still had enough self-control not to jump Matt's bones in front of her children. Because she'd meant what she'd said to him—she had neither the energy nor the inclination for a romantic relationship, even if she was suddenly, achingly aware that it had been more than a year since she'd had sex.

When Matt stepped out onto the back deck, the twins raced toward him, Shane, predictably, lagging a few feet behind his brother.

"We've got pizza!" Quinn announced.

"I hope it has pepperoni," Matt said, smiling as he took the long, flat box from him.

"Lots and lots of pepperonis," Shane chimed in. "'Cuz they're my favorite."

Matt winked at him. "Mine, too."

He glanced at Georgia, who had Pippa strapped against her chest, a diaper bag in one hand and a plastic bag in the other, then gave the pizza box back to Quinn with instructions to put it on the table in the dining room.

"Let me give you a hand," he said.

"Thanks."

"What have you got in here?" He took the grocery bag.

"Paper plates and napkins, veggies and dip, juice boxes for the boys."

"I do have plates and napkins."

"It didn't seem right to bring dinner then leave you with dirty dishes."

"I would have let you wash them," he assured her.

She smiled at his teasing, relieved that there didn't seem to be any evidence of the awkwardness she'd feared. "This way I don't have to."

When Georgia got Pippa settled on a blanket with her favorite toys, she saw that the boys were already seated at the table, eager to dig into dinner. She put a slice on each of their plates and added a few veggies—broccoli and carrots for Quinn and cucumber and red pepper for Shane.

Quinn wrinkled his nose. "Don't like veggies."

"Yes, you do," she reminded him.

He ignored the vegetables and picked up his pizza.

Matt reached into the box to take a couple of pizza slices. Then he looked at the boys' plates and, with more resignation than enthusiasm, he added some carrot sticks and cucumber slices. Georgia was grateful, because she knew that neither of the boys would protest any further about eating their vegetables if Dr. Matt was eating them, too.

She had just bit into her second slice of pizza when she heard a noise emanating from behind a closed pocket door that led to Matt's kitchen. She'd noticed the closed door earlier but had assumed he had a sink full of dirty dishes he didn't want guests to see. When the noise—a whimper?—came again, she suspected that he was hiding something much more significant than unwashed plates.

The boys were already finished eating—including their vegetables—when Matt confirmed her suspicions.

"Do you guys want to see what I've got in the kitchen?" he asked them.

"Is it ice cream?" Quinn asked hopefully.

"Sorry," Matt said. "It's not ice cream."

"I like ice cream," Shane told him.

He ruffled the little boy's hair, and Shane smiled shyly in response to the casually affectionate gesture. "Then I'll make sure I have ice cream for next time."

"Whatcha got this time?" Quinn wanted to know.

In response, Matt started to open the door. He'd barely slid the barrier a few inches when a tiny bundle of fur wriggled through the narrow opening. He held his breath, not entirely sure that this surprise would go over as well as he'd anticipated. Not that he doubted the twins' response, but their mother's reaction wasn't quite so easy to gauge.

"A puppy!" Quinn announced.

The boys were already on the floor, fussing over it. Georgia pushed away from the table to join her sons.

"Are you pet-sitting for your brother?" she asked Matt.

"No," he admitted.

Her eyes widened. "He's yours?"

"Actually—" he opened the door farther and picked up a second puppy "—they're both mine."

"Two?"

He shrugged. "Well, they were the only two left, and they're brothers."

She looked up at him, her blue eyes reflecting equal parts amusement and approval, and he felt as if his heart had actually swelled inside of his chest.

"You really are a softie, aren't you?" she said.

"I'm thinking 'sucker' is more accurate," he admitted, and bent to put the second puppy down on the floor with the first.

"What are their names?" Quinn wanted to know.

"I only just brought them home," Matt said. "I haven't had time to give them names yet."

"You hafta pick good names," Quinn told him. "Not like Fluffy or Buttercup." He wrinkled his nose in obvious disapproval of such choices.

"No Fluffy or Buttercup," Matt promised solemnly.

Shane giggled as a tiny pink tongue swiped his chin. "Finnigan," he said.

Matt's brows lifted, as surprised by the unusual suggestion as the fact that Shane had offered it.

"Finnigan?" he queried.

"And Frederick," Quinn declared.

"They're characters on a television show," she explained.

Shane looked up at him. "They're brothers."

"In that case," Matt said, "I guess the only question now is, which one is Finnigan and which one is Frederick?"

The boys were in complete agreement about the assignment of the names, and it warmed Matt's heart to see their enthusiasm about the puppies. Then he looked up and saw Georgia looking at him, and the small smile on her lips warmed every other part of him.

Chapter Nine

Since bringing the puppies home, Matt had more than a few moments when he wondered, *What the hell was I thinking?* When he saw Quinn and Shane fussing over Finnigan and Frederick, he understood that he had been thinking of this exact moment. Not that he'd brought the puppies home just to score points with the little boys, but he couldn't deny that their apparent affection for the animals had been a factor in his decision.

"A tree house and puppies," Georgia mused. "My kids are going to be spending more time in your backyard than their own."

"That's okay with me," he said, dropping his voice so that the boys couldn't hear him. "Especially if their mom comes with them."

She picked up Pippa, who had begun to fuss. "Are you flirting with me?"

"Obviously I'm not doing a very good job of it if you have to ask."

"I just don't know why you'd bother when you know I have no intention of getting involved with you."

"I know that's what you said," he acknowledged.

She lifted a brow. "You don't think I meant it?"

"I think I can change your mind."

"I think you should take the puppies and the boys outside while I clear up in here," she countered, in an obvious attempt to change the topic of conversation.

"Don't worry about clearing up, I'll take care of it later."

"Okay, then, why don't you take the puppies and boys outside so I can feed Pippa?"

And he finally grasped that she hadn't been trying to change the topic so much as she'd been trying to get him out of the house so she could have some privacy. Not that he had any objections to the sight of a woman nursing her child, but he understood that Georgia might be a little self-conscious about baring her breast in front of him, especially now that she knew he wanted her in his bed.

"Matt?" she prompted.

"Take the boys and puppies outside," he agreed. "I can do that."

So he did, and he sat on the deck watching as the boys and their canine companions ran and jumped and wrestled in the grass. He tried to remember what Liam had been like at the same age, then felt a pang deep in his heart when he recalled that his son had been gone from his life before he'd celebrated his third birthday.

Matt shoved the painful memories to the back of his mind. He'd spent far too much time wishing for what he'd lost and wondering what might have been. When he'd finally sold his condo and bought this house on Larkspur Drive, he'd promised himself that he was finished living in the past and vowed to focus on the future. Now he found himself hoping that his future might include his beautiful neighbor and her three kids.

But convincing Georgia that she wanted the same thing was going to take some work.

Much to Quinn's and Shane's disappointment, the puppies tired out long before they did.

"How come he doesn't wanna play with me no more?" Quinn asked, stroking the soft fur of the puppy that had fallen asleep in his lap.

"He's just tired out right now," Matt told him. "He's still just a baby, even younger than your sister."

"Are the puppies gonna wake you up at night?"

"I hope not," he said fervently.

"What if they do?" Quinn pressed, followed by Shane's question, "Are they gonna sleep in your bed?"

"No." His response to the latter question was firm.

"I'd let him sleep with me," Shane said. "If I had a puppy."

"I think your mom might have something to say about that," Matt told him.

"She lets me sleep in her bed when I have a bad dream," Quinn said.

Matt didn't think that excuse was going to get *him* access to Georgia's bed, but he hadn't given up hope that he would be there. Preferably sooner rather than later, because he was getting tired of cold showers.

"I wish I had a puppy," Shane said wistfully.

"A puppy's a lot of work," Matt told him. "And your mom already has a lot to do, taking care of you and your brother and your sister."

"I'd take care of the puppy. She wouldn't hafta do nothin'," Quinn vowed.

Matt couldn't help but smile in response to the fervent promise that countless boys had used on their mothers over the years—mostly ineffectively.

"I think you'd have a better chance of convincing your

mother if she saw you were willing to help out with Finnigan and Frederick every once in a while."

"I'll help every day," Quinn promised.

"Me, too," Shane chimed in.

"Well, you'll have to check with your mom on that," Matt told them. "But if you can, I'd appreciate it."

"Does that mean we're friends again?" Quinn asked.

Not too much surprised Matt, but this question did. "I didn't know we stopped being friends."

"You stopped coming over."

The little boy's matter-of-fact statement made him appreciate that you could fool some people some of the time, but you couldn't fool a four-year-old. Obviously Georgia wasn't the only member of the Reed family who had recognized his avoidance.

"There was a lot of stuff going on at the hospital," he hedged.

"Did you fix more broken arms?"

He nodded. "A couple of those. A broken femur—" he tapped the little boy's thigh "—that's the bone in there, a hip replacement, some knee arthroscopies."

"What's arrow-scope-peas?"

Matt smiled. "Arthroscopy," he said again, enunciating the word more carefully. "It's an operation that uses a tiny camera to see what's inside the joint so that the doctor can fix whatever's wrong through little cuts in the skin."

Quinn drew back in horror. "You cut people?"

"Only when necessary," Matt assured him.

"You didn't cut me," Shane said.

"Because the X-ray let me see that the bone was only broken, not out of position, so we just had to put a cast on your arm to make sure the bone wouldn't move before it was healed."

The little boy considered this explanation for a minute,

then he said, "Mommy says we can't go back in the tree house till my cast is gone."

"She's probably worried that you might fall again."

"Maybe you could talk to her," Quinn suggested hopefully. "She'd listen to you, 'cuz you're a doctor."

"Nice try, but doctor's orders do not override Mommy's rules," Georgia said, stepping out onto the deck.

Matt noticed that she'd strapped on the infant carrier again and Pippa, obviously sated and happy, was snuggled inside.

Quinn let out a long-suffering sigh. "It was worth a try."

"And you get an A for effort," she told him. "But you don't go back to the tree house until *I* say so."

Shane pouted silently.

"Now take the puppies inside," she said. "It's time for us to go home so that you guys can have a bath before bed."

"Don't wanna bath," Shane said.

"I know, because you're a four-year-old boy and dirt is your best friend, but you're going to have a bath anyway."

Shane shook his head. "Quinn's my best friend, and then Finnigan and Frederick."

"Then you shouldn't mind getting rid of the dirt," Georgia said dryly, while Matt tried not to laugh at the little boy's solemn statement.

Quinn stood up, careful not to disturb the sleeping puppy in his arms. "It's okay," he told his brother. "We can come back and see the puppies tomorrow. Dr. Matt said so."

"I said *if* it was okay with your mom," he interjected quickly, before Georgia had to remind her sons again about doctor's orders and Mommy's rules.

Shane looked up at her pleadingly. "Can we, Mommy?"

"We'll figure that out tomorrow."

Quinn's lower lip jutted out.

"But if that's not acceptable, I can say 'no' now," she suggested.

Matt had to admire the quickness with which the boy

sucked his lip back so that it was in a normal position again before she'd even finished speaking.

"I guess that's acceptable then?" she prompted.

Both boys nodded as they carried the puppies back into the house.

Georgia waited until they were out of earshot before she said, "It looks like we'll be seeing you tomorrow."

"I'm already looking forward to it."

He stayed out on the deck, watching as they made their way back to their own house and wishing that they could have stayed. Not just for a little bit longer, but maybe even forever. Because somehow, over the past few weeks, he'd fallen head over heels for Georgia and her three adorable children.

He winced as tiny claws pressed down on his bare foot. He glanced down to see Finnigan—or was it Frederick?—trying to climb up his leg, wanting some attention. He scooped the puppy up and tucked him into the crook of his arm. Almost as soon as he had done so, his canine sibling appeared.

As Matt retreated back into the house with the puppies in his arms, he was consoled by the fact that he wouldn't be completely alone tonight.

Georgia didn't get much sleep that night, and she couldn't even blame Pippa because her baby girl had actually slept for almost five hours straight. Unfortunately, even while Pippa was sleeping, Georgia was tossing and turning—thinking about Matt Garrett. *Wanting* Matt Garrett.

She wasn't used to having her hormones all stirred up, especially not by someone who wasn't her husband. She wasn't sure what to do about it, or even if she wanted to do anything at all.

Matt was stirring her up on purpose—of that she had no doubt. To an outside observer, his treatment of her had been nothing but circumspect throughout the evening. He certainly hadn't done anything obvious or inappropriate. But when he led her to the table, he placed a guiding hand at the small of her back. When he sat in his own chair, he let his knee brush against her legs. When he wanted to get her attention, he'd touch a hand to hers. And every single touch, no matter how brief or casual, made her pulse jolt and her body yearn.

She didn't know if her response was specific to her neighbor or just a symptom of the fact that she'd been celibate for so long. She suspected it was specific to Matt, because no one—before or since her marriage—had ever affected her the way he did, and she didn't have the first clue what to do about it.

She could sleep with him. That seemed the most obvious and simple answer. *If you have an itch, scratch it,* Charlotte was fond of saying. But Georgia and her mother often had differing philosophies.

And there were a lot of reasons for Georgia not to get involved with her neighbor—one of them being that he was her neighbor. If they hooked up and things didn't work out, she still had to live next door to him.

But the primary consideration was her three children. Not only did their presence complicate the situation and decrease the likelihood of finding any alone time, she had to consider how any kind of romantic involvement would affect them. She didn't doubt that Quinn and Shane would be in favor of a relationship between their mother and "Dr. Matt" because they loved hanging out with him. But if things didn't work out, how difficult would it be for them to lose that connection? They'd been devastated by Phillip's death. For weeks after the funeral, they'd been plagued by nightmares; and for several more months, they'd frequently awakened Georgia in the night just to make sure she wasn't dead, too. They'd already grown so close to Matt, and she couldn't imagine what another loss would do to them. And because she didn't know, she wouldn't let herself risk the possibility of starting something that might only end with heartbreak—for her children and herself.

But what if things *did* work out?

Georgia wasn't sure she was willing to consider that possibility; she didn't want to look too far ahead. She didn't want a relationship—even if she was increasingly tempted to explore the chemistry between them.

As for what Matt wanted...she wasn't entirely sure. He'd admitted that he was attracted to her, so she was pretty sure he would go along with the sex thing. She just didn't know what—if anything—he wanted beyond that.

But the more time that passed, the more she thought about him, the more she wanted him. For a lot more reasons than the fact that his proximity made her all hot and bothered.

He was a good man. She knew that not all doctors had chosen the profession for benevolent reasons. But she didn't doubt that Matt had. It was his nature to help people, whether that meant fixing a broken bone or performing lawn maintenance or late-night taxi service. She knew he wasn't perfect—if he was, he wouldn't still be single. And while she couldn't deny a fair amount of curiosity about his marriage and divorce, she didn't feel it was her place to ask when they weren't really anything more than neighbors—even if the air fairly crackled whenever they were together.

But the physical attraction aside, he was innately kind and considerate, and he was great with kids.

He paid attention to her children. He looked at them when they were talking to him, he listened and responded to what they said, and he seemed to genuinely enjoy being with them. That alone was almost enough for Georgia to fall in love with him.

And the knowledge that she could fall in love with him was what terrified her.

If she thought she could scratch the proverbial itch and be done with it, she might have been more willing to take that next step. But she worried that scratching would only make the itch more intense—because the more time she spent with Matt Garrett, the more she wanted to be with him.

It turned out that the answer to Quinn's question was a resounding yes—the puppies did wake Matt up in the night. Three times, in fact. And each time that he was up, he noticed that there was a light shining in Pippa's room, so he knew Georgia was up, too.

A couple of times, he saw her shadow through the curtains as she passed in front of the window. He could barely keep his eyes open on night one with the puppies, so he could only imagine how exhausted she must be after more than four months of sleepless nights.

When he'd asked, Georgia told him that Pippa was sleeping better and her bouts of fussiness were less frequent and intense. Since Matt couldn't hear the baby crying, he figured that was probably true, but he still didn't think Georgia was getting much sleep.

A suspicion that was proven by the shadows under her eyes when he knocked on her door late the following morning.

"I was just going to take Finn and Fred for a walk and thought the boys might want to come with me," he said.

"We want to," Quinn responded before his mother could.

"Pippa's just gone down for a nap," Georgia told him.

"Why don't you do the same?" Matt suggested.

"You're going to take two boys and two puppies by yourself?"

"Don't I look capable?"

"It's not your ability I doubt, it's your desire."

Even before his lips curved, her cheeks filled with color as she realized how her statement could be interpreted.

"I thought we answered that question definitively the other night," he teased.

"I meant your willingness to take a walk with two boys and two puppies."

"I'm willing—and capable," he assured her. "And we won't be gone too long."

She looked down at the hopeful faces of her sons. "Go get your shoes."

The twins raced down the hall to the closet, and Matt took advantage of their temporary absence to dip his head and kiss their mother. It was a brief touch, barely more than a brush of his lips against hers. Certainly not enough to satisfy him, but enough to thoroughly fluster Georgia.

Before she could say anything, the boys were back.

"We're ready," Quinn said.

Matt took each boy by the hand. "Then let's go get the puppies."

Georgia intended to take advantage of the boys' absence to get some work done. But after checking her email and replying to the messages that needed replies, she found herself struggling to concentrate. And it was Matt Garrett's fault—even when he wasn't around, she couldn't seem to get him out of her mind.

She'd always been extremely focused and never, in her entire life, had she let herself be so easily and completely distracted by a man. Not that she was "letting" herself be distracted now—she just couldn't stop thinking about him.

And it wasn't just because she had let the twins go off with him. In fact, she wasn't the least bit worried about her children with Matt, because he'd proven that he was more than capable of looking after the boys and she absolutely trusted that he would do so.

But while she wasn't worried about her children, she was worried about herself. Because somehow, Matt Garrett had taken hold of her heart and she didn't have the first clue what to do about it.

The slap of the screen door against its frame jolted her back to the present.

"Mommy?"

"In the dining room," she said.

Quinn raced into the room, his brother on his heels and Matt right behind them, looking completely at ease with her children—and far too handsome and sexy for her peace of mind.

"We tired the puppies out," her son told her proudly. "Dr. Matt had to carry them home 'cuz they were too tired to walk."

"Then you guys must be pretty tired, too," she said, ruffling her son's hair.

"Nuh-uh," Shane said. "We're goin' for ice cream."

She lifted a brow. "Ice cream?"

"You haven't heard of it?" Matt teased. "It's a frozen dairy dessert."

She rolled her eyes. "I've heard of it. In fact, I've actually tasted it once or twice before."

"But have you experienced the bliss of Walton's ice cream?"

Georgia shook her head, thinking that there were a lot of blisses she would willingly experience with this man.

"You haven't really had ice cream until you've had Walton's," he told her.

She forced herself to ignore the clamoring of her suddenly hyperactive hormones. "It's almost time for lunch." She felt compelled to point this out to all of them.

"Walk on the wild side," he suggested, "and eat your dessert first for a change."

The low, sexy tone of his voice raised goose bumps on her flesh, but she ignored the physiological response of her body and focused on more practical matters.

"If the boys have ice cream now, they won't eat their lunch."

"A kiddie cone," Matt cajoled.

"Pleeeease," Quinn and Shane chorused.

She believed it was important for the boys to understand that there were rules to follow, but she wasn't so rigid that she would never bend those rules. And though she was tempted to bend this time, she shook her head. "Pippa isn't up from her nap yet, and when she wakes up she's going to need to be changed and fed."

As if on cue, the sound of Pippa babbling and cooing came through the baby monitor.

"Pippa's up," Quinn told her.

"It sounds like she is," Georgia agreed.

"Ice cream?" Shane said hopefully.

"Let me take care of Pippa, and then we'll go for ice cream."

Because that was one blissful experience she could justify, but personal fantasies about the doctor next door she could not.

Chapter Ten

When Matt had agreed to take the remaining two puppies from his brother, he'd worried about how much time and attention they would need. Luke had somehow convinced him that having two puppies would be less work than one because they would be company for one another and content to play together. After a few days, Matt had found that was generally true. He'd also discovered that Finnigan and Frederick were never happier than when they were playing with Quinn and Shane—and the twins seemed equally enamored of their furry friends.

It was, to Matt's mind, a win-win situation. Or maybe it was a win-win-win situation, because when the boys were hanging out with the puppies, it gave him an excuse to hang out with Georgia. Since keeping a distance hadn't stopped him from thinking about her, he'd abandoned his campaign of avoidance for a new tack—spend as much time with her as possible in the hope that she would want him as much as he wanted her.

He knew she wasn't there yet, but he knew she was thinking about him. He saw it in the awareness in her eyes when he touched her, heard it in the huskiness of her voice when he stood close, and he'd definitely tasted it in the sweet softness of her lips when he kissed her.

Yeah, she was thinking about him, and hopefully—with just a little bit of a nudge in the right direction—she would be thinking about a lot more.

As they made their way toward Walton's, Georgia carrying Pippa in her baby carrier and Matt pulling the twins in their wagon, he considered that today just might be the day to give her that nudge.

"How did I not know this place was here?" she wondered, taking in the long row of freezers, the candy toppings displayed in glass containers and the list of menu items that stretched across the long wall behind the counter.

"You're new in town," he noted.

And because it was her first visit, she took her time surveying the offerings while the boys raced back and forth, pointing out one flavor then another.

Matt gave her a few minutes before he asked, "What looks good to you?"

"Everything," she said, and then she sighed. "But I'm going to have to pass."

He shook his head. "You can't come into Walton's and walk away from the counter empty-handed."

"Is that written into the local bylaws?"

"If it's not, it should be," he told her.

"I followed your advice and cut out dairy and it seems to have helped alleviate some of Pippa's colic. So as tempted as I am, I'm not going to sacrifice my sleep for a brief taste of sinful decadence."

But he heard the regret in her voice, and couldn't resist teasing, "Sinful decadence is the best reason I can think of to sacrifice sleep—but I'm not talking about ice cream."

The flush in her cheeks confirmed that she knew what he was talking about. “These days, I’m not sacrificing my sleep for *anything*.”

He just grinned and turned her toward the freezer on the other side of the counter. “Nondairy sorbets.”

She nibbled on her bottom lip, obviously tempted, as was he—but not for ice cream.

He might have been teasing when he’d responded to her comment about sinful decadence, but his desire for her was very real. There were all kinds of deliciously sinful things he wanted to do to her body, all kinds of decadent pleasures he wanted to share with her.

“The orange mango looks really good,” Georgia finally said. “But so does the piña colada…and the raspberry…and the lemon lime.”

“Raspberry gets my vote,” Matt told her. “Or you could go for the sampler bowl and try three different flavors.”

She shook her head. “I’ll stick with the orange mango for today. I have a feeling the boys are going to want to come back here on a regular basis.”

Matt ordered an orange mango cone for her and a raspberry for himself, while Georgia tried to help the boys narrow down their choices. Through the bits and pieces of conversation that he overheard, it sounded as if Quinn was vacillating between chocolate chip cookie dough, chocolate fudge brownie and chocolate peanut butter cup. Apparently the kid really liked chocolate. Surprisingly, Shane seemed to have already made up his mind.

“Two kiddie cones,” Georgia finally told the teen behind the counter. “One chocolate peanut butter cup and one vanilla.”

Vanilla? To Matt’s way of thinking, that was almost as bad as not having any ice cream at all.

“Wait.” He held up a hand to the server and turned his attention to Shane. “Vanilla? Really?”

Shane looked down at his feet, but he nodded.

"That's your absolute favorite flavor?"

"I like 'nilla," he said. But the quiet statement was hardly a rousing endorsement.

"Better than cotton candy or bubble gum or—" Matt looked at the Kids' Favorites labels "—superhero or alien invasion?"

That got the kid's attention.

Shane lifted his head. "What's alien 'vasion?"

Matt boosted him up so that he could see into the freezer case.

"It's lime sherbet with blueberry swirl and fruit juice gummies," the server said, then winked at Shane. "And one of my favorites."

The little boy nibbled on his bottom lip, considering.

"You want to give it a try or do you want to stick with vanilla?" Matt challenged.

The server scooped a tiny spoon into the bin and offered Shane a taste.

He looked to his mother for permission before accepting the spoon and cautiously sliding it between his lips. He hesitated for another minute, then pointed to the green ice cream. "That one. Please."

They decided to eat inside in the hope that Quinn and Shane might be able to finish their cones before they melted. Georgia seemed worried that, despite the sample, Shane would change his mind about alien invasion. But after a few more tentative licks, he pronounced it "the best ice cream ever" and she finally turned her attention to her sorbet—and had Matt's attention completely riveted on her.

Quinn gobbled his ice cream, as if he was afraid someone might try to take it from him. Shane—happy to have broadened his flavor horizons—worked at his cone methodically and steadily. Georgia savored every lick, closing her eyes and humming in appreciation as the sorbet melted on her tongue.

She somehow turned the consumption of a single scoop of sorbet into a blissful, sensual experience, making Matt wonder: If she was this passionate about dessert, how much passion would she exhibit in the bedroom?

"Doncha like it?"

Shane's question snapped Matt out of his reverie and back to the present.

"'Cuz you can share mine if you don't like yours," the little boy offered.

Matt shook his head. "Thanks, but I think I'll leave it up to you to gobble up all the alien invaders."

Shane smiled at that and took a bite of his cone.

The boys finished quickly—probably because they had as much ice cream on their hands and faces as in their bellies, the result of Quinn deciding to dig a peanut butter cup out of his cone in exchange for one of the gummy aliens from his brother's—and Georgia sent them to the washroom to clean up.

Though he knew it would only increase his own torture, he convinced Georgia to sample his raspberry, and nearly groaned aloud as he watched the tip of her tongue lap delicately at the sorbet. But when he tried to finagle a taste of her orange mango, she refused.

"You said the raspberry's the best," she explained. "Which implies that you've already tried every flavor."

It was true, but her obvious enjoyment of the orange mango made him suspect that it might taste better than he'd remembered. But since she wasn't sharing, he leaned over and touched his mouth to hers.

"Mmm." He swiped his tongue over her bottom lip. "Maybe that is better than the raspberry."

She drew back and when he shifted, as if to kiss her again, she stuck the cone between them to keep him at a distance.

He nibbled at her sorbet; she narrowed her gaze.

"You think you're clever, don't you? Tricking me into letting you taste my sorbet."

"The sorbet was my consolation prize—what I really wanted was a taste of you."

"You got that, too, didn't you?"

His gaze dropped to her mouth. "Not nearly enough."

Georgia and Matt finished their cones and they headed back outside. Pippa was still comfortably snuggled in her baby carrier, so as soon as the boys had climbed back into their wagon, they were ready to head out. She automatically reached for the handle of the wagon, only to find that Matt had beat her to it.

He kept telling her that she didn't have to do everything on her own, and Georgia was starting to believe it. But as nice as it was to have someone around who was willing to lend a helping hand, Matt had done so much for her already and Georgia didn't want to let herself rely on him too much.

She'd always prided herself on her independence. If she didn't count on anyone else, then she wouldn't ever be disappointed. But she found that she was starting to depend on Matt, not just because he helped her out in so many ways, but for his company and conversation. She liked having him around, just knowing he was there.

And the more time she spent with Matt, the more that growing attachment concerned her. And it wasn't only her own feelings that she was worried about.

"You're awfully quiet," Matt noted. "Something on your mind?"

She shook her head, unwilling to admit that *he* was the reason for her preoccupation. But after a moment, she realized there was something else bothering her, too.

"Shane always has vanilla," she said.

"Did I overstep by suggesting that he try something different?"

She shook her head again. "No. I'm just surprised that he was willing. His dad was strictly a vanilla guy," she admitted. "And I think one of the reasons Shane always had vanilla was a subconscious attempt to be more like his dad."

That maybe having something in common would cause Phillip to pay more attention to him. But of course she didn't say that part out loud. "He's always been so painfully shy, so much quieter than Quinn. Part of it, I suspect, is being Quinn's brother. My sister likes to joke that Shane doesn't talk much because he never has a chance to get a word in edgewise."

Matt glanced back at the wagon, where Quinn was entertaining his brother with a running commentary of one thing or another. "There might be something to that theory," he mused.

"Maybe," she acknowledged with a smile. "But he's talked more to you in the past three weeks than he's talked to anyone else in the past three months."

"Is that good or bad?" he asked cautiously.

"It's good." Now she looked over her shoulder at the boys in the wagon. "Spending time with you has been good for both of them."

"And yet you say that as if it's a bad thing," he noted.

She sighed. "I just don't want them to start expecting too much, depending on you."

"Because I'm not dependable?"

"Because they're not your responsibility."

"Why does it have to be about responsibility?" he demanded. "Why can't I just hang out with you and your kids because I enjoy hanging out with you and your kids?"

"You're twisting everything around," she protested.

He paused in the middle of the sidewalk. "*I'm* twisting things around?"

"Yes. I'm just trying to establish some boundaries—"

"And every time you throw up boundaries, you only tempt me to breach them," he warned, deliberately dropping his gaze to her mouth so she knew that he was thinking about kissing her again.

Georgia had spent more than enough time remembering every minute detail of their first kiss and, with her lips still tingling from the much briefer but more recent kiss in the ice cream parlor, she decided it would be smart to heed his warning.

"I'll keep that in mind," she promised.

Satisfied by her response, he started walking again.

Georgia fell into step beside him, as baffled as she was intrigued by this man. But it was a nice day for a walk, so she tried to concentrate on the scenery rather than her frustrating neighbor.

She'd always scoffed at the idea that people moved faster in the city. Life in New York hadn't seemed so fast when she was moving at the same frenetic pace as everyone else. Whenever she and Phillip had gone out anywhere, they'd rushed to the subway so the underground train could whisk them to their destination. They'd always been in a hurry to get where they were going. As odd as it seemed, she couldn't even remember just taking a leisurely stroll with her husband.

For a lot of reasons, she'd been reluctant to leave Manhattan. She hadn't wanted to take the boys away from everything familiar, but she'd felt so isolated and alone in the city. Maybe Phillip hadn't been a very hands-on dad, but he'd at least been there so she wasn't completely on her own. When he'd died, she'd become painfully aware of how truly alone she was. And with three-and-a-half-year-old twins and another baby on the way, she'd also felt completely overwhelmed.

When Charlotte left for Vegas, Georgia had been alone again, although not for long. Matt had moved in next door and suddenly she had a neighbor, a friend, a confidante... and maybe even more.

And she wanted more, even if she wasn't ready to admit it.

For the past year, she'd focused on being a mother to the exclusion of almost everything else. Being with Matt made her remember that she was a woman, with a woman's wants and needs.

She just hadn't yet figured out what, if anything, she was going to do about those wants and needs.

Five days later, Georgia still didn't have any answers. Since four of those days had been Matt's days at the hospital, she didn't see much of him. It was just like the man to get her all stirred up and then disappear, and she didn't doubt for a single minute that he'd done it on purpose. He was giving her time to think, to wonder, to want. She could no longer deny that she wanted.

But while she'd spent the better part of four days thinking about Matt, he'd apparently been busy planning a party, because when she took the boys outside late Saturday afternoon, there was quite a crowd gathered on his back deck. Even from a distance, she recognized both of his brothers and a woman that she thought might have been Kelsey, but most of the other guests were unfamiliar.

"Finnigan and Frederick are out," Quinn said, already heading in that direction.

Georgia caught his arm just before he raced past her. "I know you want to see the puppies but you can't just go over to someone else's house uninvited."

"Dr. Matt said we could go anytime," Quinn reminded her.

"I know that's what he said, but he has other company today and it isn't polite to intrude."

"I don't wanna be polite," her son protested. "I wanna see Finn."

She had to fight against a smile. No matter his faults, at least he was honest.

"I'm sure you'll see Finn tomorrow, and the day after that, and the day—"

"I wanna see him today!"

And apparently the puppy wanted to see him, too, because before Georgia could admonish her son, the puppy came tearing across the grass, racing as fast as his little legs could carry him. As usual, Fred was right behind him, neck-in-neck with a third puppy.

"Look, Mommy." Shane's eyes were wide. "Finn and Fred have a friend."

"I'm thinking he might actually be another brother," Georgia said.

Finnigan and Frederick were ecstatic to be reunited with their pint-sized playmates, and they jumped and danced around the twins while their companion went exploring. He put his nose deep in the grass and followed a trail—directly to Pippa's blanket.

Georgia watched as the baby and puppy eyed one another. Pippa lifted a hand, as if to touch him, and the puppy pulled back, out of reach. She dropped her hand, he moved closer, sniffed her face, then swiped his tongue across her chin. Pippa giggled.

The puppy licked her again; the baby giggled some more.

And then a strong arm reached down and scooped the puppy up and away. Pippa tipped her head up, wondering where her furry friend had disappeared to, and smiled when she saw him wriggling in Luke Garrett's hold.

"I'm so sorry," Matt's brother apologized. "I didn't think he would venture too far—or so quickly."

"No worries," Georgia assured him. "And he might not have ventured this way on his own, but he followed Finn and Fred."

"I should have been keeping a closer eye on him, so he didn't slobber all over your child."

She shrugged. "A little doggy spit never hurt anyone."

"I wish you could tell that to my date from last night."

Georgia's brows lifted. "She had a different opinion?"

"Oh, yeah," he told her. "When I took her back to my place after dinner—"

She held up a hand. "I'm not sure I want to follow wherever you're going with this."

Luke grinned. "Strictly *G*-rated. All that happened was Einstein licked her hand—not even her face, just her hand. And just once. And she jumped up screaming 'I've got dog germs' like Lucy in the old cartoons."

She couldn't help but smile at the image his words evoked. "First question—how did you end up dating a woman who doesn't like animals?"

"It was a blind date," he said. "I didn't know she didn't like animals."

She didn't even ask about the fact that he'd taken a woman, on a first date, back to his place. Obviously a lot of things had changed since the last time she'd been on a first date. Instead, she said, "Second question—Einstein?"

He sighed. "Because he's not."

"Having a little trouble training him?"

"More than a little," he admitted. "I have never met an animal so determined not to do what he's told."

"Wait until you have kids."

He shook his head. Emphatically.

"Not that I dislike kids," he hastened to explain. "And yours are great. I just don't see myself as a father—not anytime in the near future, anyway."

"That's because he's still a kid himself," Matt said.

Georgia hadn't seen her neighbor approach, and her heart gave a little jolt when he winked at her now. And she wasn't the only female affected—Pippa's eyes lit up and she gave him a gummy smile.

Matt picked up the little girl, who settled comfortably in his embrace, and Georgia realized that her boys weren't the only ones getting attached to "Dr. Matt." And she wondered again how it was that a man who so obviously doted upon children didn't have half a dozen kids of his own.

"Undeniably," his brother admitted with a grin.

"Then I would guess that's a family trait," Georgia noted. "As common as the broad shoulders and brown hair."

"We're not as similar as people think," Luke denied. "Matt's the smart one, Jack's the charming one, *I'm* the good-looking one."

She chuckled at that. "I think you all got more than your fair share of brains, charisma and looks."

"And they're all heartbreakers," Kelsey warned, joining their conversation.

Matt tugged on the end of her ponytail. "Don't you be telling tales out of school," he warned.

"I wouldn't dream of it," she said sweetly. Then she spotted the puppy in the crook of Luke's arm. "Ohmygoodness—he is such a sweetie."

"You had your chance to take one," the vet told her.

"I've already taken enough animals off of your hands," she retorted, stealing the puppy from him—at least for the minute. "Is this one Finnigan or Frederick?"

"That one's Einstein," Luke said.

"He's sooo adorable." She tore her gaze away from the puppy for a minute to explain to Georgia, "Brittney was dying to see Uncle Matt's puppies, so I brought her over and crashed the party."

"It isn't a party," Matt protested.

"Tell that to the dozen other people hanging out on your back deck."

"I didn't invite any of those people," he denied.

"I did," Luke admitted. "Think of it as an impromptu housewarming."

Georgia glanced over at Matt's deck. "None of those people look like Brittney."

"She's in the house, on the phone with her ex-boyfriend, attempting to remind him of the 'ex' part," Kelsey told her.

Georgia winced. "That's awkward."

"Yeah. Almost as awkward as not inviting your neighbor

to a backyard barbecue," she said with a pointed glance in Matt's direction.

"I would have invited my neighbor if I'd been planning a barbecue," he retorted, before turning to Georgia to say, "Apparently I'm hosting an unplanned barbecue."

"Apparently," she agreed, trying to hold back a smile.

"So—" he nudged her playfully, caused tingles to dance down her spine and toward all of her erogenous zones "—do you want to come over for a burger?"

When he looked at her the way he was looking at her now, she was almost ready to admit that she wanted a lot more than a burger. But she wasn't going to get into that kind of conversation in front of his family and friends.

Instead, she forced herself to match his casual tone and said, "Yes, I think I do."

He held her gaze for another minute, then turned to call out to Shane and Quinn. "Come on, boys. Let's go get lunch."

Chapter Eleven

The twins were racing across the yard before Matt finished speaking.

"I remember when Brittney was that young—and that active—and wishing I could figure out a way to bottle that energy," Kelsey said to Georgia.

"I wish the same thing," she agreed. "Every single day."

Matt wanted to be part of her every single day—to share the joys and responsibilities of raising a family with her. But as much as he wanted it, the prospect also scared the hell out of him.

After the failure of his marriage, he'd thought he might never heal, and he'd vowed that he would never give his heart to anyone again. Somehow, over the past few weeks, Georgia and her kids had stolen it away from him. And he didn't know whether to be frustrated or grateful that she didn't seem to have a clue.

Luke's elbow jamming into his ribs severed his wayward

thoughts. "Since you've got your arms full of adoring female, I'll take Finn and Fred back to the house."

Matt nodded and glanced down at the little girl in his arms. He didn't know if she was adoring, but she was absolutely adorable, and gazing up at him with big blue eyes just like her mother's. And just like her mother, she had firmly taken hold of his heart.

Luke and Kelsey headed back across the yard with the puppies, while Georgia gathered up Pippa's supplies. By the time she and Matt made their way across the yard, Jack had the food line moving. Hot dogs and hamburgers were available at the barbecue and an assortment of potluck dishes were set out on the picnic table. Brittney—having finally ended her conversation with Brayden—held Shane's plate so that he could load it up. Like his brother, he opted for the hot dog with a side of macaroni salad and homemade baked beans.

"Beans are awesome!" Quinn declared. "They make you fart real loud!"

Though everyone chuckled—even Adam, the baker of the beans—Matt saw the color rise in Georgia's cheeks, the natural blush making her eyes look even bluer than usual and somehow more beautiful.

By the time she settled Pippa in her bouncy chair and they joined the food line, the boys were half finished with their meals. Matt introduced Georgia to various guests who passed by: Adam Webber and Melanie Quinlan; Tyler Sullivan; Tyler's brother, Mason, and Mason's wife, Zoe, and their kids; Gage and Megan Richmond and their three-year-old son, Marcus.

"And there's Megan's sister—"

"I'm never going to remember everyone," Georgia warned him.

"—Ashley Turcotte and her husband, Cameron."

But she smiled as the couple drew nearer. "I'll remember those names, because Dr. Turcotte is our new family doctor."

"I'm only a doctor when I'm wearing the white coat," Cameron said, protesting her use of his formal title.

"Or when there's a scraped knee in the vicinity," his wife added, offering her hand.

"I'm Georgia Reed."

"The city girl with the three kids who moved in next to Dr. Garrett," Ashley noted.

"He moved in next to me," Georgia pointed out, with just a hint of exasperation in her tone.

The other woman chuckled. "I know, but the rumor mill always orbits around the locals."

"Which is just one more reason to be glad you're an import," Matt told her. Then, to Ashley, "Where are Maddie and Alyssa?"

"Our daughters discovered your tree house."

"Have they eaten?" Cameron asked.

"Maddie said that they needed to go exploring to work up an appetite first," his wife explained.

"Those are my boys," Georgia told Ashley, pointing out the twins who were seated on a blanket with Brittney. "They always seem to have an appetite."

"But their mom needs to eat, too," Matt said, nudging Georgia toward the barbecue where Jack had a long-handled spatula in one hand and his own burger in the other.

"Make sure you try Zoe's broccoli salad," Ashley advised.

Matt and Georgia loaded up their plates and found a couple of empty chairs near Brittney and the twins. A few minutes later, Kelsey and her husband, Ian, joined them. And when everyone had a plate, Jack finally abandoned the grill and came over.

"Hey, Britt, I heard Matt talked you into playing on our softball team for the Fourth of July tournament," he said.

"Despite my protests and against my better judgment," she said. "Which I'll remind you again when I strike out for the umpteenth time."

"We've got three weeks to practice—we'll get you hitting the ball," he said confidently.

The teen shook her head. "I really suck, Uncle Jack."

"I'm sure you're not that bad." Kelsey tried to assure her daughter.

"Actually she is," Luke said, dropping onto the blanket beside the twins.

Brittney wadded up her napkin to throw it at him—and missed her target by a mile.

He winked at her. "Thanks for proving my point."

"You can show her how it's done at practice tomorrow," Matt told his brother.

"Three o'clock at the park," Jack confirmed.

"There's swings at the park," Shane said.

"And monkey bars!" Quinn added.

"Do you guys want to go to the park?" Brittney asked.

They both nodded enthusiastically.

She looked at their mother. "Do you mind if I take them over there for a while?"

"They would be thrilled and I would be grateful," Georgia told her.

"Why don't we round up all the kids and I'll go with you?" Luke offered. He looked at Jack, as if he expected to rope him into babysitting duty, too.

Jack shook his head. "I'm going to check the food supply, make sure no one goes hungry."

Ian stood up. "Actually, I could go for another burger."

"Me, too," Matt said, then he turned to Georgia. "Do you want anything?"

"Brittney to live with me so she can keep the boys entertained 24/7?" she asked hopefully.

"You'll have to talk to her mother about that," he said, heading back toward the barbecue.

Georgia turned to see Kelsey was already shaking her head. "Sorry, but Northeastern has dibs."

"But not until September, right?"

"Not until September," she agreed, then sighed. "Damn, I'm going to miss her."

"I can imagine," Georgia admitted. "The boys are only starting kindergarten in the fall, but already I'm thinking about how quiet the house will seem when they're at school."

"Don't blink," Kelsey warned. "Because before you know it, they'll be packing their bags for college."

Georgia watched the boys, each one holding on to one of Brittney's hands, with a trail of other kids behind them. They were in their glory, not just because they had Brittney's attention but because there were other kids to play with, too.

"I'm not accustomed to anything like this," she told Kelsey.

"Like what?"

"Big, noisy get-togethers. Growing up, it was just my mom and my sisters and I. Obviously, I didn't know what I was missing."

"You mean the chaos and confusion?" Kelsey teased.

Georgia smiled. "No, that came along with the twins. What I meant was the camaraderie, and the sense of comfort that comes from knowing that there's always someone there. Matt and his brothers might argue and tease one another mercilessly, but there's no doubt that each one would go to the wall for the others."

"And they have," Kelsey confirmed. "You don't have that kind of relationship with your sisters?"

Georgia shook her head. "Maybe it's geography—I'm here, Virginia's in Texas and Indy's in Alaska."

"That's a lot of distance," the other woman noted.

"I sometimes wonder if we went our separate ways because we never had a sense of belonging anywhere."

"It makes a difference," Kelsey agreed. "Matt and Jack and Luke all went away to school, but they all came back to Pinehurst in the end."

"How about you?" Georgia asked.

The other woman shook her head. "My sister was the one with wanderlust. I never wanted to be anywhere else."

"I had mixed feelings about moving to Pinehurst after my husband died. But now, I'm so glad that I did. This is what I want for my children—a home in a community where everyone looks out for their neighbors."

"Is that a diplomatic way of saying 'where everyone butts into everyone else's business'?"

"That thought never once crossed my mind."

Kelsey laughed, because she saw right through the lie. "So tell me, now that you've accepted we're all busybodies, what has Matt said or done that has you worried?"

Georgia wasn't usually the type to confide in a woman she barely knew, but she didn't know many people in Pinehurst and she desperately needed someone to talk to. And Kelsey seemed a more logical choice than the elderly Mrs. Dunford.

"He kissed me," she admitted.

"And that surprised you?"

"Maybe not the kiss itself," she admitted. "But the intensity of it."

"Matt's never been the type to do anything by half measures," Kelsey said. Then, after a beat, she asked, "How was it?"

Just the memory of that kiss had Georgia's blood humming. "Beyond spectacular."

The other woman grinned. "Go Matt."

"That's the problem," Georgia said. "I don't know if I'm ready for this...attraction...to go anywhere."

"You're deluding yourself if you think you can stop it."

Georgia frowned at that.

"You're thinking about the kids," Kelsey guessed. "'What if I get involved with this guy and things don't work out?'"

She nodded, surprised that a woman she barely knew could be so attuned to her thoughts and concerns. Except that Kelsey was a mother, too, so maybe it wasn't surprising at all.

"Pippa's probably young enough that you don't have to worry about her too much, but the boys are already looking at Matt as if the sun rises and sets in him, and what will happen if things don't work out and he's not part of their lives anymore?"

She blew out a breath. "You're good at this."

Kelsey shrugged. "I'm a student of human nature—and I can see the situation a little more clearly because I'm not personally involved.

"I can also tell you," she continued, "that Matt isn't the type of guy to play fast and loose with anyone's heart. Despite my teasing, he wouldn't have invited you here tonight, with his family and his friends, if this wasn't where he wanted you to be."

"Or maybe he just figured I'd be less likely to complain about the music if I was invited to the party."

"You really don't see it, do you?"

"See what?" she asked warily.

"How completely smitten he is."

"He's been a good friend—"

Kelsey snorted.

"—and he's absolutely terrific with the kids."

"I've never known a man better suited to being a father or more deserving of a family," the other woman said. "Which is why I know Matt would never risk everything we just talked about if he wasn't sure he wanted a future with you."

"I think you might be reading too much into the situation."

Kelsey just smiled. "He already loves your kids, Georgia. When are you going to figure out that he's more than halfway in love with you, too?"

"No." She shook her head. "Now you're definitely reading too much into things."

"And that instinctive panicked reaction is probably why he hasn't told you how he feels," Kelsey said.

Then she gathered up the empty plates and headed up to the house, leaving Georgia alone to think about what she'd said.

She decided that just because Kelsey and Matt were good friends didn't mean that the other woman knew what was in his heart. Certainly he'd never given any indication that he was "halfway in love" with her, or even "completely smitten." Sure, he flirted with her, and he'd kissed her once—okay, a few times, but the more recent kisses had been too quick to really count, even if she'd felt tingles all the way down to her toes—but he hadn't given any indication he wanted to take things any further than that.

She wanted to put Kelsey's words out of her mind, but her gaze kept zeroing in on Matt as she watched him mingle with his friends, and she couldn't help but admire his easy manner. She also couldn't help but admire the way his shorts hugged his spectacular backside, and felt that now-familiar throbbing in her veins. There was no doubt about it, Matt Garrett was a fine specimen of masculinity.

It was only Pippa's fussing that succeeded in tearing her attention away from the doctor next door, and she ducked into the house to find a private corner to nurse her. When the baby was finally sated, Georgia rejoined the group that had gathered on Matt's back deck. With all the other kids at the park with Brittney and Luke, Pippa was the star attraction, and she was happy to let herself be passed from one set of arms to another, charming all with her big blue eyes and even bigger smile.

Georgia was chatting to Adam Webber—a fifth-grade teacher at the school the boys would be attending in the fall—when Matt made his way back to her. Adam, catching a look from the host, excused himself to grab another drink. When he did, Matt stepped into the space his friend had vacated and slipped an arm around Georgia's waist.

She eyed him warily. "You're going to give your friends the wrong idea about us."

He nuzzled her ear, and she couldn't quite suppress the delicious shiver that skated down her spine. "I'm trying to give you the *right* idea about us."

"You haven't listened to anything I've said, have you?"

"I've listened to a lot of things you've said," he countered. "But all your protests about not wanting to get involved can't override how right you feel in my arms. Or the fact that your body's instinctive reactions contradict your verbal responses."

She just sighed. "I don't know what to do about you."

"I have a few ideas," he teased. "But I'm not sure you're ready to hear them just yet."

"We're *friends,*" she said firmly.

"Believe me, I'm feeling very friendly right now."

She shook her head, but she couldn't help smiling. "You are far too charming for your own good."

"The Garrett curse," he lamented.

"I'll bet it is."

Somehow, Georgia was still there when the rest of Matt's guests had cleared out. The twins had played for hours outside—first with the puppies, then at the park with Brittney and the other kids, then with the puppies again—until they were as tired out as their four-legged friends. Georgia had wanted to take them home to get them ready for bed, but they'd balked at that idea. When Matt suggested they could go inside to watch TV, they'd jumped all over that offer with both feet.

Pippa was awake again, but happily playing with the soft toys attached to her bouncy chair. Her fussy nights finally seemed to be a thing of the past, for which Georgia was immensely grateful. But while Georgia was getting more sleep, she wasn't feeling any more rested because her sleep continued to be disturbed by erotic dreams starring one very handsome doctor.

"I didn't think they would ever leave," Matt said, as the last car pulled out of the driveway.

"You have an interesting group of friends," she noted. "Have you known them all very long?"

"Most of us go back to grade school," he admitted.

"Really?"

"Why do you sound so incredulous? You must keep in touch with friends you went to school with."

She shook her head. "There were too many schools to keep track from one year to the next. In fact, it was rare for me to walk out of class in June at the same school I'd started in September."

"Was your father in the military?"

"No, my mother was following her bliss."

"Really?"

"She's settled down in recent years—or so I thought until I got the phone call informing me that she'd found husband number five."

"Where's your dad?" Matt wondered.

"Somewhere in Atlanta."

"Is that why you're named Georgia?"

She nodded. "And I have a half sister named Virginia and another half sister named Indy."

"Short for Indiana?" he guessed.

"No, she was actually named for the Indy race circuit. Her father was a member of one of the pit crews and we traveled so much from track to track that summer, Charlotte couldn't be sure whether the baby had been conceived in Wisconsin or Iowa, so she decided to go with Indy."

He smiled. "A good choice, considering the other options."

She nodded her agreement. "Charlotte always said the only

crime in life is in not following your heart wherever it wants to lead."

"And you disapprove of that philosophy?" he guessed.

"I didn't see that following her heart ever led to anything more than heartache."

"Did you never follow yours?"

She glanced away. "I believe the desires of the heart need to be balanced against the reason of the mind."

"How long did it take you to balance the desires of your heart with the reason of your mind when your husband proposed?" he teased.

"He never actually proposed."

"He never proposed?" Now Matt was the one who sounded incredulous.

"The topic of marriage came up in conversation and we decided it was what we both wanted, so we got married. The formalities weren't as important as being together to either of us."

He shook his head. "Next you're going to tell me that you got married at city hall."

"What's wrong with that?"

"Not a thing—if that's what you wanted," he said.

She'd told herself that it was, that she didn't need a white dress or a bouquet of flowers. She wasn't the type to be influenced by romantic trappings or swayed by amorous words. She wasn't like her mother.

But there had been a few occasions—usually other people's weddings—when she found herself wishing they'd done things a little differently. Not that she'd ever admitted it to anyone, and she wasn't going to do so now. Instead, she stood up. "I should check on the kids."

She'd set the twins up in the living room to watch a program on the Discovery Channel, but now they were both fast asleep.

"I hope this isn't a premonition," she murmured to Matt, who had followed her into the house.

"Of what?"

"Their attention span for educational instruction. I don't want them falling asleep in class when they start kindergarten in September."

"I don't think you need to worry. They just crashed because they had an incredibly busy day."

She nodded, acknowledging the point. "But regardless of how exhausted they were, if I'd put cartoons on TV, they'd still be awake."

"Which is obviously why you didn't put cartoons on."

But now that they were asleep, she was second-guessing her choice. Because Quinn and Shane were supposed to be her chaperones, and she was suddenly conscious of being *un*-chaperoned with her sexy neighbor. "I should get them home."

"You're going to wake them up to take them home so they can go to sleep?"

"They should be in their beds," she insisted.

"They seem comfortable enough," he noted.

Looking at her boys cuddled up with the puppies, Georgia couldn't disagree. But that didn't make her any less uneasy.

They moved into the kitchen, where their conversation wouldn't disturb the kids, and Matt said, "I should have considered that you might be tired. How are you holding up?"

"I didn't do anything all day. Your brother cooked the burgers, your friends supplied the rest of the food, Brittney occupied the boys, and everyone else took turns with the baby." She looked up at him and smiled. "In fact, I was thinking we should do it again tomorrow."

The implication of her words registered too late, and she immediately tried to backtrack.

"I didn't mean to imply… I mean, I don't expect you to spend all of your free time hanging out with me and my kids."

Matt just shook his head. "When are you going to figure out that I like hanging out with you and your kids?"

"It's starting to sink in," she told him.

"Maybe this will help," he said, and lowered his mouth to hers.

Chapter Twelve

Matt prided himself on being a patient man. When he'd decided that he wanted Georgia—about three minutes after their first meeting—he'd accepted that it would probably take her some time to come to the same realization. He also figured there was no harm in nudging her in that direction.

He braced his hands on the counter, bracketing her between them, and brushed his lips over hers softly, slowly. Her eyes fluttered, closed. He traced the shape of her mouth with just the tip of his tongue. She breathed out a sigh.

Apparently she didn't need as much nudging as he'd anticipated, because when he swept along the seam of her lips, they parted willingly. His hands moved from the counter to her hips; her palms slid over his chest, her hands linking behind his neck.

He deepened the kiss, stroking the inside of her mouth with his tongue. He didn't demand a response but coaxed it from her. Their tongues danced together in a sensual rhythm of advance and retreat that had all the blood rushing from his head. Part of him felt as if he could go on kissing her for hours, but another part refused to be satisfied with kissing.

His hands moved up her rib cage, over her breasts. She moaned and pressed closer. This was exactly how he wanted her—warm and willing in his arms. His hands curved around her bottom, pulling her tight against him. He was rock hard and aching with wanting her, and she was rubbing against him, her movements so natural and sensual she nearly pushed him to the brink.

Determined to regain control of the situation, he eased his lips from hers to trail kisses across her jaw, down her throat. He nipped at the nape of her neck, and she shuddered against him. His tongue traced over her collarbone, then along the edge of the lacy cup of her bra. Her skin was so soft, her breasts so perfect and round, and when he nuzzled the hollow between them, he could feel her heart racing.

He brushed his thumbs over her nipples, and she shuddered again. But when he reached for the clasp at the front of her bra, she pushed his hand away, shaking her head.

Reminding himself that he'd promised to be patient, he didn't push back. Instead, he cupped her face in his hands.

"What are you afraid of, Georgia?"

"I'm not sure," she admitted.

"I'm not going to push for more than you're ready to give," he promised.

Her smile was wry. "Maybe that's what I'm afraid of. Because there's a pretty big disparity between what my body wants and what my brain is thinking."

He brushed his lips against hers. "Would it be wrong for me to encourage you to listen to your body?"

"Believe me, my hormones are clamoring loudly enough without any encouragement."

"At least you're no longer trying to deny the chemistry between us."

"That would be hypocritical, considering the way I was pressed up against you less than a minute ago."

"I liked the way you were pressed up against me," he assured her. "In fact, feel free to press up against me anytime."

She shook her head. "That was a temporary state of mindlessness induced by an overload of hormones after more than a year of celibacy."

"Is that what you think it was?" He had to fight to keep his voice level, his tone casual. "Just a combination of factors that really had nothing to do with you and me?"

Her gaze shifted away. "It seems like the most reasonable explanation."

"Then let's be unreasonable," he suggested, and lowered his head again to nibble on her bottom lip.

His efforts were rewarded by a soft moan low in her throat.

"I can be unreasonable," she agreed.

Which sounded like a green light to Matt.

He allowed his hands to stroke over her shoulders, down her arms, while he continued to kiss her. Deeply. Hungrily. And she responded with equal passion.

His hand slipped down the front of her shorts, dipped inside her panties. She gasped as his fingers sifted through the soft curls in search of her womanly core. He had to bite back his own moan when he found her hot and wet and oh-so-ready.

He slid a finger deep inside of her, and let his thumb zero in on the tiny nub of her most sensitive erogenous zone. She moaned again but made no protest as he slowly and inexorably coaxed her closer and closer to the pinnacle of her pleasure.

She was mindless now, writhing and panting. He didn't disagree that hormones played a role in what was happening here, but he knew that it was more than that. And he wanted more than hot, meaningless sex—he wanted intimacy. From the first, he'd sensed that deeper level of connection with Georgia, and he'd be damned if he'd let her dismiss what was between them as nothing more than a transitory urge.

He slid his finger in again, then two fingers. In and out, deeper and faster now, while his thumb continued to stroke her nub. He felt the clamp of her inner muscles around his fingers in the exact moment that her teeth sank into his bottom lip, the unexpected shock of erotic pleasure nearly bringing him to climax. He clamped his other arm around her waist, holding on to her, while the shudders racked her body.

She eased her lips from his and dropped her head against his chest. But several minutes passed before she said anything, and then it was only, "Oh. My. Wow."

He managed to smile, though his own body was screaming for its own release. And when she reached for the button of his shorts, her fingertips brushing the top of his aching erection, it took more willpower than he knew he possessed to stop her.

But he caught her hands in his, held them at her sides. "It's late. You should be getting home."

She just stared at him, stunned. "But don't you want to… finish?"

"What I want," he told her, "is to take you upstairs, slowly strip every piece of clothing away, and spend hours touching and kissing you all over until you're begging for me."

She swallowed. "So why…are you sending me away?"

"Aside from the fact that your screams of pleasure might wake your kids?"

Her cheeks flushed. "I guess that's a good reason."

"But the main reason," he continued, "is that I'm not going to make love with you until I know it's what you want, too. Not because you need a release, but because you want *me*."

She glanced away, but not before he saw that her eyes had filled with tears. Cursing himself, he put a hand on her arm.

Not surprisingly, she shrugged away from his touch.

"Should I thank you for taking the edge off?"

Except that there was still an edge—he could hear it in her voice.

"It wasn't all for you," he said, because it was true. "Touching you was definitely my pleasure."

But she turned away, proving that his words hadn't swayed her. "I need to get the kids home."

He held back a sigh. After all, he was the one who had reminded her it was getting late.

"You take Pippa, I'll bring the boys."

She opened her mouth as if to protest, because even now, she didn't like to accept help from anyone.

"Unless you really want to make three trips," he said.

"Thank you—I would appreciate your help." Except that her sharp tone and narrowed gaze contradicted her words.

She slung Pippa's diaper bag over her shoulder and lifted the bouncy chair with the baby securely fastened and contentedly slumbering in it. It was a little more awkward for Matt to juggle the twins without waking them up, but he managed.

He kicked off his shoes inside the front door and carried the boys upstairs to their bedroom while Georgia changed Pippa. He ignored the pajamas that were neatly folded at the foot of each bed and laid Quinn gently on top of his mattress.

He'd done this before—tucked a sleeping child into his bed. And while the memories of his son usually tore at his heart, tonight—with Georgia's little boy cuddled up against his chest—he was able to smile at the remembrance.

Then he eased Shane down onto his pillow and carefully tucked the covers around him. He brushed away a lock of hair and impulsively touched his lips to the child's forehead.

"Night-night, Daddy."

Matt froze.

He'd always wanted to be a father, and even after he'd lost Liam, he'd been confident that he would have other children someday. But he hadn't realized how much he wanted to be a father to Georgia's kids until he heard the word *Daddy* slip from Shane's lips. He knew the little boy was asleep, and that the words had been murmured subconsciously, but that knowledge didn't prevent them from arrowing straight to his heart.

He took a moment to compose himself before he moved back to Quinn's bed, tucked his covers around him and kissed his forehead. He wasn't sure if he was relieved or disappointed when this twin didn't stir.

Georgia was just leaving Pippa's room when he stepped into the hall. She followed him down the stairs.

"Thank you," she said formally. "For helping with the boys and for inviting us to dinner."

"You're welcome," he said.

And because he couldn't resist, he touched his mouth to hers, softly, fleetingly.

She kept her lips tightly compressed, but her lack of response didn't faze him. Because he knew now, without a doubt, that she wanted him as much as he wanted her.

Now he just had to wait for her to come to the same realization.

He was driving Georgia insane.

Six days after Matt had given her an up-close-and-personal glimpse of the stars and the heavens, he was acting as if absolutely nothing out of the ordinary had happened. Then again, maybe arousing women to the point of climax in his kitchen wasn't out of the ordinary for him. But it had been an extraordinary experience for her—and an incredibly frustrating one.

She hadn't meant to insult him when she'd tried to explain away the sizzle between them as a basic physiological response to their proximity. It made sense to her that more than twelve months of celibacy in combination with post-pregnancy hormones would fuel an attraction to the sexy doctor. But Matt had taken exception to her reasoning and endeavored to prove that what she wanted wasn't just sex but sex with him.

And he was right, damn it. Because when she went to

sleep that night, she didn't dream about hot, sweaty sex with nameless, faceless partners, she dreamed about hot, sweaty sex with Matt Garrett. And she woke up craving his kiss, aching for his touch, yearning for the fulfillment she knew only he could give her.

Since Phillip had passed away, she'd been a mom first and foremost. She'd been dealing with the twins' grief and her own pregnancy. She hadn't missed sex—in fact, she hadn't even thought about it. For more than a year, it was as if every womanly urge in her body had simply shut down. And then Matt Garrett had moved in next door.

Being around him stirred all kinds of wants and needs inside of her. He made her feel like a whole woman again. Except that, in the past six days, nada. Not one kiss, not the brush of a single fingertip on her skin, nothing.

Not that he was avoiding her. In fact, she was practically tripping over him every time she turned around. He was solicitous and helpful and he continued to spend a lot of his free time with the boys. He'd even taken it upon himself to make a trip to the local garden center and arranged for a delivery of sand to fill the empty box at the back of her mother's yard. And he was out there with the boys now, driving dump trucks, bulldozers and cement mixers through the sand right alongside them.

Yeah, he was having a great time with the boys, and he hadn't made a single move to touch her or kiss her in six days. At first she'd thought he was punishing her, then she started to wonder if he'd lost interest, maybe he'd decided that she wasn't worth the effort. Except then she'd catch him looking at her, and the intense heat of his stare certainly didn't telegraph disinterest.

Stepping outside, she called to the boys. "Quinn, Shane—lunch is ready."

The boys jumped up, wiping their sand-covered hands on their shorts before they raced toward the house. Matt followed behind them, at a more leisurely pace. While the boys went inside to wash up, she waited for her neighbor.

"I made a pot of chili, if you wanted to join us."

"Thanks, but I've got some things I have to do."

She stepped in front of him, blocking his path. "Are you going to stay mad at me forever?"

"I'm not mad at you," he told her.

"Then why haven't you kissed me in six days?"

The corner of his mouth tilted up in a half smile. "You've been counting the days?"

She lifted her chin, met his gaze evenly. "Have you changed your mind about wanting me?"

The answer was evident in his eyes before he spoke. The glint of amusement in his gaze immediately replaced by desire—hot and hungry and unrestrained. "No," he said slowly. "I haven't changed my mind."

"So why haven't you kissed me?"

"Because I was afraid that if I started, I wouldn't be able to stop."

She swallowed. "Maybe I wouldn't want you to stop."

He took a step back. "Let me know when you can make that statement without the 'maybe.'"

"I'm sorry," she said with a sigh. "I'm not playing hard-to-get. At least, not on purpose."

His smile was wry. "I know."

And then he pressed a quick kiss to her lips.

It was almost too quick, and he was walking away before the fact even registered in her brain. But it had certainly registered in her body, zinging through every nerve ending from the tip of her head to the soles of her feet and everywhere in between.

If she thought about it, she might have worried that her response to the casual touch was too much. But in the moment, all she could think was that she wanted much more. That she wanted him to kiss her and touch her and never stop.

But she wasn't ready to say the words out loud. And even if she was, it was too late.

He was already gone.

A few days later, Georgia decided to reward herself for finishing her reports on three slush pile submissions with a trip to the park. Since the boys had mostly behaved and let her focus on her work, she decided to take them with her. It wasn't until they got to the park and she saw Matt in the outfield that she knew his team—the Garrett Gators—was practicing today.

While the boys played—Shane no longer encumbered by the cast that had been removed the day before—she put Pippa on her blanket on the grass. Her daughter had recently learned to roll from her stomach to her back and vice versa, and she happily spent a lot of time practicing her new skill. While Georgia was proud of her daughter, she was also a little wary. Pippa's increased mobility required even greater diligence because Georgia knew that if she turned her back for a moment, the baby might roll out of sight. For the moment, however, she seemed content just to go back and forth.

"Heads up!"

Georgia spun around to see the ball pop high into the air and over the backstop of the baseball diamond. Instinctively, she cupped her hands and snagged the ball before it dropped near the baby. There was a smattering of applause from the field as she tossed the ball back to the catcher.

"Sign her up!" somebody yelled from the field.

Georgia ignored the commentary and turned back to Pippa who had, in her mother's brief moment of inattention, rolled all the way to the edge of the blanket. With a mock admonishment, she scooped up the baby and set her in the middle of the quilt again.

"Mrs. Reed?"

She glanced up to see Brittney jogging toward her. Georgia smiled at the girl. "Another practice for the Fourth of July tournament?"

"Yeah," the teen responded with a complete lack of enthusiasm. "And I still completely suck. Unfortunately, there are strict rules about the number of men and women you can have on each team, and uncle Matt's team needed another female body on the field."

"I'm sure you'll do just fine," Georgia told her.

Brittney shook her head. "After half a dozen practices, it's still my instinct to get out of the way when the ball's coming toward me. I haven't fielded a single hit and I haven't hit a single pitch past the pitcher's mound."

"Why are you telling me this?"

"Because when that ball came at you, you didn't even think about it—you just reached out and grabbed it."

"A mother's instinct," she explained. "I was protecting the baby."

"Still, it proved that you'd be a much better asset to the team than I am," Brittney told her.

"Matt asked me if I wanted to play, but—" she gestured to the boys on the climber and Pippa on the blanket under the tree "—I can't sit them in the bleachers and expect them to stay put."

"I'd be happy to hang out with the kids if you took my spot at second base. No, I'd be *thrilled,*" the girl amended.

Still, Georgia hesitated. "I haven't played baseball in more years than I care to admit."

"Give it a try now," Brittney urged, offering her glove.

And that was how Georgia found herself playing second base for the Garrett Gators on the Fourth of July.

The local sports complex had been turned into a carnival for the holiday, including a family fun zone with an enormous ball pit, a twenty-foot inflatable slide, a puppet theatre, and face painting and balloon animals for the little kids. For the bigger kids, there was a midway area with thrill rides and games of chance and skill. And since everyone in attendance had an appetite, food vendors offered everything from hot dogs, popcorn and snow cones to perogies, schnitzel and sushi. But one of the biggest draws of the day was the Sixth Annual Co-ed Softball for Sick Kids Hospital Tournament.

Brittney's best friend, Nina, had offered to help out with the kids, but Georgia still couldn't help worrying that the twins and Pippa would be too much for the girls over the course of the day. And she was feeling more than a little guilty that she wasn't able to spend the day with her family. But the twins were happy to wander off with the teens, who pushed Pippa along in her stroller, leaving Georgia with nothing to do but play ball.

There were two divisions of three teams in the tournament, so every team played a five-inning game against each of the others in its division to determine standings. Then the two first-place teams played for the championship trophy.

Georgia nursed Pippa between games and made sure that the girls had enough money to keep the twins occupied and supplied with snacks. At the end of the first round, it was announced that the Garrett Gators would be facing off against the Sullivan Swingers for the hardware.

"A rematch of last year's final," Ashley Turcotte said, in a tone that warned Georgia that game had not ended well for the Gators.

"What happened?" she asked.

"Tyler Sullivan cranked a solo home run over the right field fence to win it for the Swingers in the bottom of the ninth."

"Ty got lucky on that one," Luke grumbled.

"And for months afterward by retelling the story to any female who would listen," Jack chimed in.

"We've got a better team this year," Matt said confidently.

"So do they," Karen, Luke's receptionist and their right

fielder, noted. "They finished with a better run differential, so they're the home team again."

"Then let's get ready to bat," Matt suggested.

Matt had always loved baseball. Hardball or softball, windmill or slo-pitch, it was a fun game. And while the annual charity tournament didn't have quite the same intensity as the high school state championship, there was definitely a rivalry between the Gators and the Swingers, and Matt really wanted payback.

This year's game, just like the previous one, was a close contest. The Gators would go up by a couple of runs in the top of the inning, then the Swingers would catch up when they batted in the bottom. And just like the previous year, the game was on the line in the bottom of the ninth when Tyler Sullivan stepped up to the plate with two outs. But this time, he didn't need a big hit. With his sister-in-law at third base, he only needed a single to score her and tie the game.

In center field, Matt pulled his ball cap lower and focused his attention on the plate. Tyler took a big swing at the first pitch, fouling it back and out of play. When the second pitch came off of his bat, Matt immediately knew by the crack of the bat that it had made contact right at the sweet spot.

Cursing under his breath, he watched the ball fly...straight at Georgia. As if in slow motion, she lifted her glove and the ball disappeared inside its pocket.

The umpire held up his closed fist to signal the final out; Tyler dropped his bat in disgust; the spectators went crazy. Matt stood still, stunned.

Georgia barely had time to toss the ball back toward the pitcher's mound before she was lifted off her feet and swung around. Jack, from his position at shortstop, had reached her first, and when he finally put her feet back on the ground, he planted a kiss right on her mouth. Luke, who had been on first, was next in line. Following his brother's example, he gave her a smack on the lips, too.

Adam Webber showed a little more restraint. After high-fiving her, he said, "I'm just glad the ball wasn't hit to third. I mean, I like all these guys, and I don't mind them patting my butt, but I draw the line at kissing."

"I draw the line at kissing you, too," Jack told him.

There were more high fives all around, and then the Gators lined up for the post-game handshakes with the Swingers.

After the trophy had been presented and the crowd began to disperse, Matt saw Tyler Sullivan approach Georgia to ask, "So what are you doing next Fourth of July?"

She just chuckled. "I don't make any plans that far ahead."

"So you're not on the Gators' permanent roster?" he pressed.

"Back off, Sullivan," Matt growled.

Tyler just grinned. "Can't blame a guy for trying."

"Are you trying to steal my second baseman or snag my woman?"

Georgia seemed as startled by the question as Tyler.

"Your woman?" she echoed.

Tyler, sensing that the fireworks might start hours ahead of schedule, held up his hands in a gesture of surrender and backed off.

Matt slipped his arm around Georgia's waist. "Any woman who can snag a line drive for the final out in the bottom of the ninth and go three-for-four at the plate is the woman for me."

"The ball was hit right into my glove and it's pretty hard to strike out when your own team is pitching to you."

"Cam managed to do it," Luke said. "Twice today."

"They were foul tips," Cam pointed out in his defense. "They don't count as a third strike in real baseball."

Ten-year-old Maddie, who had been their bat girl, patted his shoulder. "You're still a hero to me, Daddy."

He kissed the top of his daughter's head. "That's all that

matters to me." Then he draped an arm over his wife's shoulders. "That, and scoring when I get home."

Ashley shook her head, but she was smiling as they walked away.

"Speaking of scoring," Karen said, winking at Georgia. "I have to admit that I'm curious. Now that you've been kissed by all three of the Garrett brothers, which one would you score the highest?"

Georgia's cheeks filled with color, but she responded lightly, "I'm not the kind of girl who kisses and tells."

"At least tell me this—is their reputation warranted?"

She smiled. "Absolutely."

Chapter Thirteen

Thankfully, before Georgia could be pressed for more details, Quinn and Shane came running onto the field. She bent down to receive their hugs and kisses. As sweaty and dirty and exhausted as she was, just holding her boys was enough to make her forget everything else.

"You were awesome, Mommy!" Shane's voice was filled with admiration, and her heart swelled with pride.

"Better than the Yankees!" Quinn declared, because that was undoubtedly the highest praise he could think of.

"A performance that definitely warrants ice cream," Matt noted.

"Ice cream?" Quinn said hopefully.

"Well, don't you think your mommy deserves a reward after that terrific game?"

Shane nodded. "Me, too."

Matt grinned. "You bet. Ice cream for everyone. Go tell Brittney and Nina that they're invited, too."

Georgia held back a groan as the twins raced away again.

"You, too," Matt told his brothers. "If you want to join us."

But Jack shook his head regretfully. "I've got a huge file to review before a trial on Monday."

"And I just got a call from Peggy Morgan asking me to take a look at Southpaw."

"She still has that old cat?"

"Probably not for much longer," Luke said. Then, to Georgia, "Make him spring for a double scoop—you more than earned it today."

"I guess it's just you and me," Matt said to Georgia when his brothers had gone.

"And two teens, two preschoolers and an infant," she added. And then, more hopefully, "Or you could let me beg off, too."

"You don't want ice cream?"

"Right now, I just want to go home, wash all the sweat and dust from my body and crawl into bed."

"That sounds even better than ice cream," he said.

"Alone," she said pointedly.

His smile never wavered. "A doctor knows all the muscles in the human body. I'd be happy to help you work out some of the kinks."

"A tempting thought, but I think I'll pass." She tossed him the baseball glove she'd borrowed.

He caught it against his chest, then took a step closer. "Is it?" he wanted to know. "A tempting thought?"

"If you're asking if I've thought about your hands on my body, the answer is yes."

His eyes darkened. "I should have known you'd make that admission at a time and place where I can't do anything about it," he grumbled.

She smiled sweetly. "It seemed safest."

He stepped closer. "Do you want to see the fireworks tonight?"

She lifted a brow; he grinned.

"That wasn't some kind of secret code," he assured her. "The town puts on a fabulous fireworks display back here after dark. I'm sure the boys would love it."

"They probably would," she agreed. "But I don't know about Pippa."

"Brittney could keep an eye on Pippa and the puppies at my place."

"She's been watching my kids all day."

"She owes me, for bailing on the team."

"I thought you said you owed her a 'thank you' for that," she reminded him.

"I'll thank her tomorrow," he promised. "After she babysits tonight."

Of course, Georgia wouldn't really disappoint her boys by bailing on a trip for ice cream, so they all piled into her van and made the short drive to Walton's. Unfortunately, the lineup at Walton's was not short, and she suspected that everyone who'd been at the game had the same idea as Matt. But they finally made their way to the cashier and placed their orders: s'mores sundae for Brittney, hot fudge with nuts for Nina, a chocolate chip cookie dough kiddie cone for Quinn, alien invasion again for Shane—apparently he had a new favorite—lemon-lime sorbet for Georgia, and the colossal banana split for Matt.

By the time they polished off their treats and headed back home, the boys could barely keep their eyes open and Georgia knew there was no way they would stay awake for the fireworks show. In fact, she still had doubts about whether *she* could stay awake, but she owed it to Matt to make the effort.

While he went home to shower and change, she steered the boys into the bathroom and filled the tub. When they were clean and dry, she instructed them to put their pajamas on and brush their teeth while she took her turn in the shower. By the time she finished, Pippa was hungry again, so Georgia sent the boys downstairs with Brittney and Nina while she fed the baby, promising them a story when she was done.

Matt returned to find the twins hanging out with the teens, waiting for their mom to read them a bedtime story. When he suggested that he could read the story, the boys exchanged wary glances.

"Mommy tells the bestest stories," Shane told him.

"But you can read to us now," Quinn said, handing him the book he'd picked out. "'Cuz Mommy's busy with Pippa."

"All right, then," Matt agreed, and opened the book.

"Upstairs," Shane told him.

"It's not a bedtime story if we're not in bed," Quinn explained.

"I don't know what I was thinking," Matt said, and followed them up to their room.

When the boys were settled with Matt sandwiched between them—in Shane's bed tonight, because apparently they alternated and it was his turn—he opened the book again. It was a story about a funny, furry monster that had the boys giggling out loud at various parts, sometimes even before Matt read the words on the page, so he knew it was a story they'd heard several times before. By the time he got to the last page, both boys were snuggled in close and struggling to stay awake.

When he closed the cover, Shane tilted his head back to look up at him. "Maybe you could be our new daddy."

It was the hopeful tone even more than the words that squeezed Matt's heart. And he wanted, more than anything, to agree with the little boy's suggestion. But it wouldn't be smart to get Shane's hopes up—or his own—until he knew that Georgia was on board with the idea, too.

"If you were our daddy, then me and Shane could take care of Finnigan and Frederick for you all the time," Quinn said.

Matt had to clear his throat before he could speak. "Well, that's definitely something to consider."

"But you'd hafta marry Mommy to be our daddy," Quinn continued.

He was mildly amused and incredibly humbled by their reasoning. "Is that how it works?"

Both boys nodded.

"You do like her, doncha?" Shane asked.

"Yes, I like her," he admitted, fighting against the smile that wanted to curve his lips. "And I like you guys, too."

"That's good, 'cuz we like you, too."

Georgia paused just outside the door of the twins' bedroom. She hadn't intended to eavesdrop—she hadn't even known that Matt was back until she heard his voice down the hall. And she hadn't overheard much of their conversation, just enough to get the impression that they were having a meeting of the mutual admiration society.

But when Quinn said, "That's good, 'cuz we like you, too," she saw Shane shake his head. And her heart broke, just a little, when her shy son looked up at him and said, "I love you, Dr. Matt."

She'd worried that she was making a huge mistake in allowing herself to get close to Matt; she'd been even more worried about the twins. And just as she'd suspected, her boys had already given him their fragile, trusting hearts. Now she stood frozen in the doorway, waiting for him to respond to her son's heartfelt confession.

Matt lifted a hand and gently tousled Shane's hair. "I love you guys, too," he said, his voice husky with emotion.

And Georgia's heart tumbled right out of her chest to land at his feet.

Over the past couple of months, she felt as if she'd gotten to know Matt Garrett fairly well. She knew he was a dedicated surgeon who cared about his patients, a brother with close ties to his siblings, a neighbor always willing to lend a hand, and the man who made her heart beat faster whenever he was near. He was good with kids and kind to animals—and he kissed like there was no tomorrow. He was smart and sexy and far too charming. But he was also steadfast, reliable and trustworthy.

She pressed a hand to her rapidly beating heart and prayed that she wasn't wrong about that part. Because she'd decided that she was finally ready to prove that she trusted him, with her body *and* her heart.

But first she had to get her kids to sleep.

Obviously Matt was thinking along the same lines, because he said, "Now let's get you both tucked into your own beds before your mom comes in to check on you."

Quinn climbed out of his brother's bed and into his own, pulling his sheets up under his chin and closing his eyes tight.

"Well, look at this," she said, stepping into the room. "My two handsome boys with their jammies on and teeth brushed, all snuggled down and ready to go to sleep."

Quinn's eyes popped open and he exchanged a guilty glance with Shane.

"You did brush your teeth, didn't you?"

Of course she knew that they hadn't, because she'd checked their brushes on her way past the bathroom and found they were still dry.

"We forgot," Shane admitted.

"Then you better go do it now," she advised.

"But I'm already in bed and I'm really tired," Quinn protested.

"Then the hot dogs and cotton candy and ice cream on your teeth will be a delicious feast for the cavity monsters who come out when you're asleep."

She held back a smile as the boys scrambled out of bed and raced to the bathroom.

While they were brushing, she crossed the room to where Matt was standing and kissed his cheek. "Thank you."

"For what?"

"Being so great with the boys."

"They're great boys," he said, with an ease that assured her he meant it.

"I think so," she agreed, then smiled. "Most of the time, anyway."

The boys raced back into the room, stopping in front of Georgia and opening their mouths for the ritual inspection to ensure there wasn't anything left for the cavity monsters to snack on in the night.

"Looks good," she said approvingly.

Then there was a round of hugs and kisses and she tucked them into bed again. Matt glanced at his watch as he followed her into the hall, and she knew he was eager to head back over to the park. But when they made their way down the stairs and into the empty living room, he frowned.

"Where did Brittney and Nina go?"

"I sent them home." She hoped she sounded more confident than she felt, because now that they were really alone, her stomach was in such a mess of knots she didn't think they'd ever untangle.

"I thought we were going back to the park to see the fireworks."

"I changed my mind."

"Don't I get a vote?"

She shook her head. "No, but you have a choice."

"What choice is that?" Matt asked her.

She lifted her arms to link them around his neck. "You can go back to the park for the fireworks—" her fingers cupped the back of his head, drew it down towards hers "—or we can make some of our own right here."

And then she kissed him.

To his credit, it didn't take him long to catch on to the change in their plans. In the space of a heartbeat, surprise had given way to seduction. He didn't respond to her kiss so much as he took it over—and she let him, because she'd never known anyone who kissed like Matt Garrett, with singular purpose and intense focus.

His lips were firm and masterful, confident and seductive. His tongue slid between her lips, stroked the roof of her mouth. Tingles of anticipation danced over her skin, desire shot through her veins. She wanted this—wanted him—more than she'd realized. And as glorious as it was to be kissed by Matt Garrett, she wanted more. She slid her hands over his chest, where she could feel the beat of his heart beneath her palms—strong and steady. Just like Matt.

She wanted to touch him, to feel the warm texture of his skin beneath her hands. Intent on her goal, she started to tug his shirt out of his pants, and nearly whimpered in protest when he caught her wrists in his hands and held them at her sides.

She eased her mouth from his and looked up at him, her gaze steady and sure. "I want you, Matt. Now. Tonight."

His eyes darkened, as much she suspected with satisfaction as with desire, but she didn't care. He could be as smug and self-righteous as he wanted, so long as he was with her.

"No doubts?"

She shook her head. "No doubts."

His lips hovered over hers again, tantalizingly close and oh so far away. "Are you going to let me strip every piece of clothing off your body, then touch you and kiss you all over until you're begging for me?"

Georgia wondered how she'd so quickly lost control of the situation. She'd set out to seduce him, and with just a few well-chosen words spoken in that low, sexy voice, he practically had her on the brink of climax. It made her wonder what would happen when he finally touched her—and made her desperate for his touch. But before that could happen, she had to make one thing clear. "I don't beg."

He grinned. "We'll see."

He captured her mouth again, kissing her so deeply and thoroughly she wanted to beg him to never stop. He finally released his hold on her wrists, skimming his fingers up the length of her arms to her shoulders, over her collarbone. Her skin burned everywhere he touched, and her body yearned everywhere he didn't. He traced the V-neckline of her blouse, raising goose bumps on her flesh. Then his thumbs brushed over her nipples, and she moaned as sharp arrows of pleasure shot to her core.

His hands immediately dropped away. "Did I hurt you?"

"No." She shook her head and grasped his wrists, drawing his hands back to her breasts. "I love the feel of your hands on me."

"Good. Because I want to touch all of you. I want to explore every inch of your satiny skin, every dip and curve of your exquisite body." As he spoke, his hands moved over her, from her shoulders to her breasts to her hips and her thighs, making her shudder.

"Are you planning to do all of that in the middle of my living room?" she asked.

"I guess a room with a door would be a better option."

"Upstairs," she said.

"I know," he said, and scooped her into his arms.

He knew because he'd taken her to her bed once before. At the time, she'd been practically comatose and unable to appreciate having a strong, handsome man at her disposal. She was definitely going to appreciate him tonight.

And despite having told him that she never wanted a man to sweep her off her feet, she couldn't deny that there was something incredibly romantic about being held against a solid, masculine chest with a pair of strong arms around her.

He set her on her feet just inside the room, then turned and closed the door with a soft click. Then he waited, as if giving her one last chance to change her mind. She took his hand and led him over to the bed.

Her heart was racing and her knees were shaking, not because she was afraid but because she'd never wanted anyone as much as she wanted this man now. He laid her down gently on the mattress and lowered himself over her. Then he kissed her again, and she sighed in blissful pleasure.

She wasn't aware that he'd unfastened the buttons of her shirt until he pushed the fabric over her shoulders and down her arms. Then he dipped his head to kiss the hollow between her breasts before he unclipped the front of her bra and parted the lacy cups. She tensed, because her breasts were ultrasensitive as a result of nursing Pippa, and nearly lost it when he touched his tongue to her nipple.

He continued to focus his attention on her breasts, alternately licking, kissing and suckling until she was very close to begging. And then his mouth moved lower, raining kisses over her rib cage, the curve of her belly, and lower still. She tensed, her hands fisted in the covers, as he removed her jeans.

His fingers trailed along the soft skin inside her thighs, coaxing them to part. Then his tongue followed the same path to the apex of her thighs, and with the first touch of his tongue to her center, she simply and completely shattered.

"Matt." His name was both a whimper and a plea, but not even Georgia knew if she was begging him to stop—or not.

He didn't alter course. With his lips and his tongue and his teeth, he continued to tease and torment her, driving her higher and higher, ever closer to another pinnacle of pleasure. She bit down hard on her lip to keep from crying out. She wouldn't have thought it was possible, but somehow the second climax was even more explosive than the first.

"Now. Please now."

He paused only long enough to take care of protection, and her body was still pulsing with the aftershocks when he finally levered himself over and into her. She cried out as another wave of pleasure crashed over her. She didn't think it was possible, that she'd had anything left to give, but Matt proved her wrong once again. As her body found its rhythm in concert with his, she was flooded with new sensations, unimaginable pleasures.

She arched beneath him, lifting her legs to hook them over his hips, drawing him even deeper inside her. His groan mingled with hers, and he began to thrust faster, harder, deeper. Her fingers dug into his shoulders, the short nails scoring his flesh, as her body tensed again.

This time he rode the wave with her, crest after crest, until he finally shuddered his release into her.

Matt had dreamed of Georgia, hot and naked and screaming his name. But as vivid as those dreams had been, they paled in comparison to the reality of the woman in his arms. Making love with her had transcended all of his expectations. She was passionate and playful, and the result was an experience both gloriously intense and unexpectedly fun.

But the best part about making love with Georgia was that even after his body was sated, he still wanted to be with her. He wasn't proud to admit it, but he'd had a few interludes after which he couldn't wait to put his clothes back on and go home. And that, he'd finally understood, was the difference between meaningless sex and true intimacy. Both served a purpose, at least with respect to satisfying basic physiological needs, but he'd quickly grown [illegible] f attraction without affection. Thankfully, [illegible] re was plenty of both.

[illegible] is breath, he propped [illegible] resist teasing, "You

[illegible] out from the sheet as Georgia shrug[illegible]

"Oh, y[illegible] tter to you."

[illegible] traced a pat[illegible] ed a fingertip to that bare shoulder, [illegible] elow the sheet, over the curve of her breast to circ[illegible] pple. "That was the only reason?"

"That and the fact that—" her breath caught when he gently tweaked her nipple "—you made my knees weak and my head spin."

He frowned, feigning concern as he shifted his attention to her other breast. "Sounds like a serious medical condition. Maybe you should see a doctor."

She smiled at that. "You don't really expect me to let you play doctor with me, do you?"

"I don't care what you call it—" he replaced his hand with his mouth, gently licking and nibbling until she was writhing and panting "—so long as you let me play."

"I can't think...of any...immediate...objections."

His hand slid over the gentle curve of her belly to the center of her femininity. And smiled with satisfaction when Georgia's breath whooshed out of her lungs and her eyes drifted shut.

"In fact...I can't think...at all."

"I like when you don't think," he told her.

She bit down on her lower lip. "Part of me wonders if I should be insulted by that remark."

"And the other part?" he prompted.

"All the other parts are too aroused to care."

"Are you going to beg again?"

"Make me," she challenged.

And because he'd never been able to resist a challenge, he did.

Chapter Fourteen

Georgia had known that Matt would be a good lover. He was too attentive and thoughtful in every aspect of his life to be otherwise in the bedroom. Not that she had much experience for comparison. She'd never been with anyone but Phillip, and she didn't know if that was the kind of admission she should have made to a potential lover.

She didn't know what Matt's expectations were when he took a woman to his bed. All kidding aside, the man did have a reputation. He'd dated a lot of women, probably slept with a lot of women—women who were likely more sophisticated and experienced than she. And women whose bodies didn't bear the evidence of having carried three babies.

She wouldn't trade any one of her children for anything in the world, but that didn't stop her from wishing—at least in the moment—that her hips were a little less round and the skin on her belly a little more taut. But Matt didn't seem to have any issues with her body during their two intense rounds of lovemaking. Which might explain why she was so thoroughly exhausted—three games of baseball followed by energetic bedroom activities would wear out anyone.

Georgia stretched her arms up over her head, trying to ease some of the kinks out of her body. Rolling over to face the other side of the bed, she was surprised to find it empty.

Obviously Matt had decided to go home, and while she was undeniably disappointed, she figured it was for the best. They really hadn't talked too much before they'd fallen into her bed, so it was probably wise for them both to take some time to think things through and reestablish boundaries. Because there had been absolutely no boundaries when she'd been naked in his arms.

After a quick trip to the bathroom, she noticed that soft light was spilling out of Pippa's partially closed doorway. Tiptoeing closer to peek into the room, she saw Matt in the rocking chair, feeding Pippa a bottle.

He'd pulled on his pants but not bothered with a shirt, and the sight of her baby girl cradled against his solid, masculine chest took her breath away. He should have looked ridiculous—a half-naked man in the midst of all the ultra-feminine décor; instead, he looked perfect—as if he belonged there.

"I raided your freezer stash again," he explained, whispering so as not to startle the baby.

"I can't believe I didn't hear her fussing."

"She didn't make too much noise," he assured her.

"You should have woken me up."

"I figured it was at least partly my fault that you were so exhausted, and I wanted to let you sleep."

Even before tonight, even before she'd watched him with her boys, she'd been more than halfway in love with him. But she'd refused to admit it, so sure that she could control her emotions. Then she'd made love with him, and she'd tumbled the rest of the way.

Now, seeing him here with Pippa, looking every bit as if he belonged there, made her wish that Matt Garrett could be a part of her life—and her children's lives—forever. Except that there had been too many stepfathers in and out of her life for Georgia to let herself even hope. Nothing was forever, and the sooner she put an end to such foolish fantasies, the better.

As he rose to put the sleeping baby back in her crib, Georgia turned away so he wouldn't see the shimmer of her tears. But he was somehow attuned to the change in her mood, because he followed her into the hall and tipped her chin up, forcing her to meet his gaze.

"What's going on, Georgia?"

She shook her head. "Nothing. You're right—I'm just really tired and…I think you should go now."

He seemed more amused than offended by her impulsive suggestion. "Where do I have to go?"

"Home."

"Why?"

The gentle patience in his tone made her want to scream. How could he be so calm when she was on the verge of a full-scale panic?

"Because it's late," she snapped.

He smiled at that. "I don't have anyone waiting up for me."

"The puppies," she suddenly remembered, seizing upon the excuse. "Don't you have to let them out?"

"I already did," he told her.

"Won't they be scared, alone in the house without you?"

"They'll be fine," he insisted, and drew her into his arms. "What I want to know is why you're suddenly scared to have me in your house with you."

"I'm not scared," she lied. "I just think we should take a step back."

His amusement faded. "You want to take a step back?"

She nodded. "Sex is sex, but sleeping together implies a certain level of intimacy."

"Yes, it does," he agreed. "And I intend to spend the night

with you, Georgia—to sleep with you in my arms and wake up with you in the morning."

She wanted that, too, far more than she should. Because if she let him stay tonight, she would want him to stay the night after that and the night after that, and eventually she would start to count on him being there.

"Do you want me to beg?" His tone was deliberately light, but she could tell by the intensity of his gaze that he understood this was a big deal to her.

"Would you?" she wondered.

His gaze never wavered. "I would do anything for you, Georgia. Don't you know that by now?"

"I guess I do," she finally said. "And maybe that's what scares me."

"Have there been so many people in your life who have let you down?"

"Each of my mother's four husbands, including my own father. Every single one of them claimed to want her and her kids, and every single one of them dropped out of our lives."

"And then your husband did the same," Matt noted with surprising insight. "Not that it was his choice, but the result was the same. He promised to be with you forever, and then he was gone, leaving you alone and your children without a father."

She nodded.

"And if even he didn't stick around, why should you trust that I will?"

She nodded again. "And before you point it out, yes, I know that I was the one trying to push you out the door."

"Because then it would be *your* choice," he noted.

Even she hadn't consciously understood the rationale behind her actions, but now she realized he was right. Every time her mother had walked out on one of her husbands, it had been Charlotte's choice, and her daughters had no option but to follow her out the door.

"Okay, you get to decide," he said. "Do you want me to stay—or do you want me to go?"

She should have been relieved that he was letting her choose, because her choice was already made. Except that somehow, during the course of their conversation, she'd started to question the wisdom of her decision to push him away. He'd proven that he understood her as no one else ever had, and he wanted to be with her anyway. And the fact that he had enough faith in her to put the choice in her hands gave her the courage to trust her heart.

She reached for his hand and linked their fingers together. "Stay."

Matt understood how hard it was for Georgia to say that single word. Because while it might have seemed like an easy response to a simple question, he knew that it was much more than that.

For Georgia, admitting that she wanted him to stay was the equivalent of putting her heart directly in his hands. And he was both grateful and relieved that she'd found the courage to do so, because whether she knew it or not, his heart was completely in hers.

This time when he took her back to bed, he showed her with his hands and his lips and his body the words he knew she wasn't ready to hear. And in the morning, when he woke with her in his arms, he had absolutely no doubt that this was how he wanted to wake up every day for the rest of his life.

Over the next several days, they resumed their normal routines with only a few minor adjustments—the puppies' bed was moved into Georgia's kitchen in the evening, he spent the nights in Georgia's bed, and she'd stopped pretending that she didn't want him there.

But as much as he enjoyed the new physical aspect of their relationship, he also enjoyed just being with her. There was so much he didn't know about her, so much he wanted to learn, and they often stayed awake late into the night just talking.

One night, after filling her in on the exploits of Finnigan and Frederick during a recent trip to Luke's office for their nine-week checkup, Georgia commented, "You've got a great relationship with your brothers, but I've never heard you mention any other family."

"That's because both of my parents died a few years back."

She winced. "I'm sorry—I shouldn't have pried."

"It's hardly a big secret," he said, and certainly not in comparison to the other, bigger secret that he'd yet to confide. Not because he didn't want to tell her, but because he knew that the time and place of the telling were crucial to ensuring her understanding, and this was not the time or the place.

Then when? the nagging voice of his conscience demanded.

Followed by Georgia's question: "Can you tell me what happened?"

It took him a second to comprehend that she was referring to the loss of his parents and not the failure of his marriage. "After my dad retired, they decided they wanted to see the world—the Great Wall of China, the Australian outback, the Serengeti—and they were having a great time. Then they decided to sail around Cape Horn, but the captain's years of experience were no match for the storm that capsized their boat. My parents—and all the crew—drowned." She took his hand, a silent gesture of comfort and encouragement.

"That must have been horrible for you and your brothers—losing them both at the same time," she murmured.

He nodded. "It was hard to find solace in anything under those circumstances, but once we'd started to get over our frustration and grief, we were able to take some comfort in the fact that they were together. Because we knew that, after almost forty years of marriage, neither one of them would have wanted to go on without the other.

"Losing them so unexpectedly was tragic," he continued.

"But we were lucky to have been witness to such an example of a strong and stable marriage, to have seen, day in and day out, the evidence of their deep love and enduring affection for one another."

"My mother has never found that kind of forever-after love," she told him. "And not for lack of searching. Yet she still believes it exists."

"It does," he said, and lowered his head to press a soft kiss to her lips.

"Did you think you'd found it with your wife?"

He leaned his forehead against hers. "Are you trying to kill the mood?"

"I guess I'm just curious," she said. "I can't imagine that you would get married without believing it was forever, and— believing it was forever I can't imagine you ever giving up on your vows. At least not easily."

"It wasn't easy," he admitted, resigned now to spilling the whole sordid story of his ex-wife's deception.

Except that the puppies suddenly broke into a chorus of yelps and howls.

Georgia froze. Matt threw back the covers and swung his legs over the edge of the mattress, but she grabbed his arm, halting his movements.

In the midst of all the frantic puppy sounds, the muttering of a female voice could be heard. Matt couldn't actually make out the words, but he thought they sounded like, "You'd think she could have told me about the dogs."

"You stay here," Georgia said, reaching for her robe. "I'll go."

He shook his head, baffled that she would even suggest such a thing. "There's someone in the house, and there's no way—"

"It's not just someone," she interrupted. "It's my mother."

Georgia had faced more than a few curveballs in her life, and having Charlotte Warring-Eckland-Tuff-Masterton-

Kendrick-Branston show up unannounced and in the middle of the night was only the latest one.

The puppies heard the creak of the stairs before Charlotte did, and they happily abandoned the unfriendly stranger in favor of the human who occasionally fed them dinner and took them for walks. Georgia bent to pat them both on their head, reassuring them that they were excellent watchdogs, before she addressed her mother.

"This is a surprise, Mom."

Charlotte kissed each of her daughter's cheeks in turn before she offered a smile that was wide, and just a little bit forced.

"Well, that was my plan—to surprise you. But I didn't mean to wake you up, baby girl," she said, a note of apology in her voice. "And actually, I don't think I did, it was the dogs. Why didn't you tell me that you were turnin' the house into a kennel?"

"It's only two puppies, and they're not mine."

"Then why are they here?"

"I'm helping out a friend," she hedged. "Why are you here?"

"As far as I know, this is still my house."

"You know it is," Georgia agreed. "But why are you showing up here at two o'clock in the morning?"

"Because it's nearly a three-hour drive from the airport," she said, as if that explained everything.

"Okay," Georgia said, trying not to lose patience. "Why did you choose to make the trip from Montana at this particular point in time?"

"I was just missin' my grandbabies so much I simply couldn't wait another day to put my arms around them, so Trigger bought me a plane ticket and here I am."

There was something about Charlotte's explanation that struck Georgia as a little off, or maybe it was the deliberately casual tone that tripped her radar. Whatever the reason,

Georgia was suddenly convinced that there was more to this impromptu trip than her mother needing a baby fix. And she was pretty sure she knew what it was.

"You left him, didn't you?"

"What are you talkin' about?"

"Trigger—your husband. The one who made you feel a jolt as if you'd stuck your finger in a socket," Georgia reminded her.

Charlotte pressed a perfectly manicured hand to her chest, right over her heart. "It was just like that," she agreed.

"So where is he now?"

"At his ranch, of course. He couldn't just abandon his animals 'cause I had a whim to see my baby girl and her babies."

"You're actually sticking to that story?"

"Really, Georgia May, I don't understand why you're being so confrontational."

Upstairs, she could hear Pippa starting to fuss, wanting to be fed, and Georgia was eager to get to the baby before her mother decided to trek up the stairs.

"I'm sorry. Maybe we should continue this conversation in the morning—or rather, at a more reasonable hour in the morning."

"Sounds good to me," Charlotte agreed. "It's been a long day and I could definitely use some shut-eye."

Georgia nodded, though she didn't expect that she would get to sleep any time soon. First she'd have to feed and change Pippa, then when the baby was settled back down and she was sure that Charlotte was asleep, she'd have to get Matt out of the house. She didn't doubt he would balk at being shoved out the back door but even though she was thirty-one years of age, Georgia still wasn't willing to risk her mother catching a man in her bed.

Another soft coo drifted down the stairs, followed by a chattier babble that was the little girl's version of a conversation. Which meant that Matt had heard the baby and, knowing that Georgia was occupied downstairs, had gone in to Pippa's room to check on her.

"Oh, the baby's awake," Charlotte said, her voice filled with genuine pleasure. "I have to take just a little peek—"

"Why don't you wait until morning?" Georgia suggested. "If she sees you now, she won't settle down again."

Charlotte waved a hand dismissively as she started up the stairs. "Don't be silly. She'll settle down just fine if she's tired."

Short of physically restraining her mother, Georgia knew there was no way to prevent Charlotte from going into Pippa's room. Which meant there was no way that she wasn't going to cross paths with—

"Matthew Garrett," Charlotte said, her voice tinged with both surprise and approval. "I was wonderin' whose size-thirteen shoes I nearly tripped over downstairs."

"Well, that wasn't as awkward as I thought it might be," Matt said, after Georgia had finished nursing the baby and Charlotte had gone back to the main floor master bedroom.

"It felt plenty awkward to me," Georgia told him.

"You're just embarrassed because your mom gave you two thumbs up before she said good-night," he teased.

"The fact that she approves of our involvement does make me wary," she admitted. "My mother has notoriously bad taste in men."

"Are you saying that because her exes were of questionable character or because the relationships were unsuccessful?"

"I'm not sure the distinction really matters."

"Sure it does. If she truly made poor choices, then you should be wary. But if they were good men, then there could be any number of reasons that things didn't work out."

"Like her habit of bailing whenever a relationship hits a snag rather than trying to find a solution?" she suggested.

"That could be an issue," he agreed.

"I don't think she's here for a visit," Georgia finally said. "I think she left Trigger."

"Wouldn't she have told you if that was the case?"

She shook her head. "No. Not until she's figured out a way to spin it so that it isn't her fault."

"That's kind of harsh, don't you think?"

She sighed. "Maybe. And maybe I'm wrong. I honestly I hope that I am, because if she did walk out on her marriage, her heart is completely shattered but she won't let anyone know it."

"I guess that proves you come by your tough demeanor honestly enough."

"You think I'm tough?"

"On the outside," he said. "On the inside, you're all soft and gooey like a marshmallow." He lowered his head to kiss her, softly, deeply. "And very, very sweet."

"Mmm." She hummed her approval as she linked her arms around his neck. "You're trying to distract mc, aren't you?"

He slid his hands beneath her shirt and unfastened the front of her bra so that her breasts spilled into his hands. Her breath hitched; her nipples pebbled. He rubbed his thumbs over the taut peaks, making her moan. "Is it working?"

Her breath shuddered out between her lips as he nibbled on the lobe of her ear. "Is what working?"

Smiling, he lowered her onto the bed.

Matt got called in to the hospital early the next morning, leaving Georgia to face her mother's barrage of questions and unsolicited advice alone. And Charlotte didn't disappoint. In fact, Georgia had barely begun cracking eggs into a bowl when her mother said, "You picked a good man, baby girl."

Considering that Matt hadn't moved in until after her mother had left for Vegas, she had to ask, "How do you know?"

"There's no disputing the Garrett boys were all players in

their youth, but everyone in town agrees that they've grown into fine, upstanding citizens. Or at least Matt and Luke," her mother clarified, a slight furrow in her brow. "There seems to be some difference of opinion with respect to Jack."

"That's your source of information—town gossip?"

"News—good and bad—travels fast in Pinehurst. And I've heard nothin' but good things about Matt Garrett." Charlotte dropped her voice, as if revealing confidential information. "Did you know that he's a doctor?"

She focused on whisking the eggs and ignored the fact that her mother actually thought Georgia might sleep with a man without knowing something as basic as his occupation. "Yes, I know he's a doctor. In fact, he put the cast on Shane's arm when he broke it."

Her mother nodded. "Smart, charming and very handsome. It's almost too much to hope that he'd also be good in bed."

"Mom!" Georgia felt her cheeks burn hotter than the skillet on the stove.

Charlotte smiled. "Well, well. My baby girl's discovered that there's passion in her blood."

"A true revelation after having three children delivered by the stork," Georgia said dryly.

"The earth doesn't have to move for a woman to get pregnant," her mother pointed out as she gathered plates and cutlery for the meal. "And while I never doubted that Phillip was a good man, I did wonder if he was a good husband."

Georgia was baffled by the statement. "Why would you ever wonder about that?"

"Because I never saw him look at you the way Matt looks at you—and vice versa."

Georgia hated to admit that it was probably true. In so many ways, she and Phillip had been well suited, but while they'd shared a certain level of attraction, they'd never generated any real sparks. Certainly nothing that could compare to the kind of sparks that flew whenever Georgia and Matt were together, but acknowledging that fact—even to her mother—seemed disloyal somehow. "I loved my husband."

"I know you did," Charlotte said. "But do you love Matt?"

She pushed the eggs around in the pan. "I've only known him a couple of months."

"I only knew Trigger a couple of days," Charlotte reminded her. "But that was long enough to know that I wanted to spend the rest of my life with him."

Except that, for some inexplicable reason, she was here and her husband was in Montana. But Georgia wasn't going to get into that with her mother today. Instead, she only said, "I'm not ready to make that kind of leap."

"Well, don't wait too long," Charlotte advised. "If you don't snap up that sexy doctor quick, another woman will."

"If he let himself be snapped up that easily by someone else, then maybe I'm better off without him."

Charlotte huffed out a breath, unable to dispute her daughter's logic, and Georgia took advantage of her momentary silence to call the boys to the table.

They were just settling down to eat when the doorbell rang. Not just once but three times in rapid succession, and then, before Georgia could even push her chair back, a fist was pounding on the door.

A quick glance across the table revealed that her mother's face was whiter than the napkin she'd twisted around her fingers. Since she obviously had no intention of going to the door, Georgia did, pulling it open to a tall, broad-shouldered cowboy, complete with hat and boots. "Can I help you?"

The man on the porch swiped the Stetson from his head, revealing neatly trimmed salt-and-pepper hair. "I'm Henry Branston. I'm here to get my wife."

Chapter Fifteen

"Your driveway's starting to look like a rental-car agency," Matt commented to Georgia when he got home from the hospital later that afternoon.

"I know. I walked to the grocery store with all the kids today because it was easier than moving three vehicles around. That and it allowed me a brief opportunity to escape from the drama."

"You can always stay at my place," he offered. "If you want some extra space."

"I might take you up on that if they don't go back to Montana soon, because after all the accusations and tears were done and they'd kissed and made up, they went straight down the hall to her bedroom and locked the door. And then I heard *noises*." She shuddered at the memory.

"Does that mean they've worked things out?" he asked cautiously.

"I think so. But what's even more bizarre, from what I

overheard of their argument, I think I understand why she left. I don't agree with her decision, but I understand."

"Want to explain it to me?"

"My mother felt as if she was the only one who made any kind of sacrifice when they got married. She left her home and her family and moved to an environment completely unfamiliar to her in order to be with the man she loved. And the more time she spent in Montana, the more she recognized that his life hadn't changed at all.

"She didn't necessarily want him to make any changes, she just wanted to know that he loved her enough to be willing to do so. The fact that he dropped everything to follow her halfway across the country to take her back home seemed to prove to her that he did love her enough."

"And now everything's okay?"

"Apparently."

"So when are they heading back to Montana?"

"Probably not soon enough," she said.

He chuckled. "As long as they're not leaving today, then I don't have to change our plans for tonight."

"Our plans?"

"Last night, when you were nursing Pippa, your mom offered to babysit the kids so that I could take you out on a real date."

She lifted a brow. "Have we had fake dates?"

He nudged her with his shoulder. "You know what I mean."

"Actually, I'm not sure that I do," she admitted. "What is a real date?"

"Dinner in a restaurant that doesn't have a kiddie menu, a movie that isn't a cartoon."

"Those things are beyond my realm of experience," she warned.

"Are you willing to give it a try?"

"We could," she allowed. "Or we could order pizza with spicy sausage, hot peppers and black olives, and watch a movie on the TV in your bedroom."

"You're assuming I have a TV in my bedroom," he pointed out.

Her lips curved. "If you don't, I'm sure we could find something else to occupy the time."

He decided to go with her plan, but upgraded it a little by setting the table with candles and champagne flutes filled with sparkling grape juice. And for dessert, he picked up some miniature pastries from the Bean There Café.

After the pizza had been eaten, Matt asked Georgia if she had any update on her mother's plans.

"They want to stay for two weeks," she told him, making the "two weeks" sound like "forever."

"Charlotte misses her grandchildren," he guessed.

"I think she does, but it was actually Trigger's idea to stay for a while, to get to know his new family." But she didn't sound very enthusiastic about the prospect.

"And you're afraid that if you get to know him, you'll like him, and if your mother walks out a second time, you might never see him again."

"That's certainly been the history," she admitted. "But honestly, I think Trigger is different. I think my mother could walk out a dozen times, and he'd track her down and take her back, because he loves her."

"Does that mean you now believe they did fall in love over a baccarat table?"

"It seems that I do."

"Then it wouldn't be completely out of the realm of possibility that a man could fall in love with his next-door neighbor after only a couple of months?"

She picked up her juice, sipped. "I guess not, but I'm hardly an expert on the subject."

"Okay, as a non-expert, do you think there's any chance that she might someday feel the same way?"

She nibbled on her lower lip for what seemed like an eternity while he waited for her response.

"I think it's possible that she already does," she said, and he was finally able to release the breath he'd been holding.

"I know you probably think I'm rushing things—even I thought I was rushing things," he admitted. "But Charlotte convinced me that sometimes the heart just knows what it wants."

"You're taking relationship advice from a woman who's been married five times and divorced four?"

"It takes courage to follow your heart."

"Then she has to be the bravest woman I know."

"She probably is," Matt agreed.

"And you think I'm a coward."

"I think you're wary," he said. "And I understand why you would be."

"My kids are my priority."

"I don't have a problem with that," he assured her. "And I don't think your kids have any problem with us being together."

"They don't, because they want you to be their new daddy. But they've already lost one father—how will they feel if things don't work out?"

"I'm thirty-eight years old and long past the stage of wanting to sow any wild oats. I wouldn't be with you—I wouldn't risk getting close to your kids—if I wasn't serious." He put his hand in his pocket and closed his fingers around the box from Diamond Jubilee. He set it on the table in front of her. "Very serious."

Georgia's breath caught when she recognized the logo. Matt hadn't opened the lid, but that didn't matter. She didn't care if he'd chosen a diamond solitaire or a cluster of cubic zirconias, it was the significance of the box itself that had her mind reeling.

"This isn't how I planned to do it," he told her. "But I couldn't let you continue thinking this is just a fling, because it's not. Not for me."

"I kind of liked the idea of a fling," she said, keeping her tone light and her hands clasped together. "I've never had one before."

"Because you're not the type of woman to share your body without giving your heart. At least, I hope you're not."

That heart was pounding frantically now, though she didn't know if it was with excitement or apprehension. "I'm also not the type of woman who believes that an intimate relationship has to lead to a walk down the aisle."

"And I've never felt compelled to propose to a woman just because I slept with her," he pointed out. "But I've been married before and if the failure of that marriage taught me nothing else, it at least taught me that there are no guarantees in life.

"After the divorce, I learned to appreciate every moment—and I vowed that if I was ever lucky enough to find someone with whom I wanted to share those moments, I would never let her go." He reached across the table and linked their hands together. "I want to share all of my moments with you."

The heartfelt words brought tears to her eyes. And while she could appreciate that he was putting it all on the line, she was too cowardly to do the same.

"I wasn't ready for this," she protested. "I'm *not* ready for this."

He released her hands and tucked the box back into his pocket. But removing it from the table didn't make her feel any less pressured, because now she knew it was there.

"I wasn't pushing you for an answer. Not right now," he said. "I just wanted you to know that I was looking toward a future for us—all of us—together."

"And I was looking forward to tonight—just the two of us."

She could tell that he was disappointed in her response, but she didn't know what else to say. Or maybe she was afraid to admit what was in her heart. She wasn't just wary—she was terrified, because what she felt for Matt was so much bigger than anything she'd ever felt before.

"Then let's start with tonight," he said, and led her upstairs to his bedroom.

Georgia wouldn't have thought it was possible, but she was almost more nervous now than the first time they'd made love. Because then she'd had no hopes or expectations beyond that single night. And when one night had become two, she'd still been content to live in the moment.

I want to share all of my moments with you.

As Matt's words echoed in the back of her mind, Georgia knew without a doubt that she wanted the same thing. From this moment to forever.

He paused in the act of unbuttoning her shirt. "You're trembling," he noted.

She could only nod.

"It can't be nerves," he said, in a gentle, teasing tone. "Because I've seen you naked at least once or twice before."

"But I never knew it wasn't just a fling before."

"But you know it now?"

She nodded again. "You matter to me, Matt. And I don't want to screw this up."

"You won't," he assured her.

"How do you know?"

"Because we're in this together, and I won't let anything screw this up for us." He kissed her then, softly, deeply, thoroughly. "I love you, Georgia."

She wasn't sure if it was the kiss or his words, but suddenly her head was spinning and her knees were weak. Her fingers curled into the fabric of his shirt, holding on. "Show me."

So he did. With each kiss, every touch and every caress,

with his lips and his hands and his body, he showed her the depth and truth of his feelings. She had never felt more treasured or cherished. Her pleasure was his pleasure. He gave and gave until she couldn't take any more, until she didn't want anything—not even her next breath—as much as she wanted him inside of her.

And when their bodies finally joined together, Georgia knew that their hearts and souls were equally entwined.

Afterward, when she was snuggled against his chest waiting for her heart rate to return to normal, she appreciated that this was one of those moments he'd been talking about. A moment that she wanted to share with only Matt. Not just because they'd had earth-shattering sex together, but because, when she was in his arms, she felt as if she truly belonged there. And because there was nowhere else in the world that she would rather be.

And along with that certainty came the courage to finally admit what she wanted. "Was there really a ring in that box you pulled out earlier?"

"You want to see it, don't you?" His lips curved, just a little. "It's always about the bling, isn't it?"

"No, I don't want to see it," she denied. "I want to wear it. But only if I hear a proper proposal." It really hadn't mattered to her that Phillip had never formally proposed. But he was her past and Matt was her future—and she wanted this time to be different. She wanted this time to really be forever.

His brows quirked. "Does that mean I have to get dressed?"

She shook her head. "It only means you have to ask."

He leaned over the edge of the mattress, searching for the pants that had been discarded on the floor to retrieve the box from the pocket. He fumbled a little, trying to open the lid, but she covered his hand.

"The proposal," she reminded him.

"Now *I'm* nervous," he admitted.

She smiled, relieved to know that she wasn't the only one. "Would it help if I told you that I'm probably going to say yes?"

"Probably?" he echoed. "That's not very reassuring."

"Well, I can't say anything until you ask the question."

"I really didn't plan to do it like this. I wanted to have all the right words to tell you how much you mean to me, how just knowing you has changed my life and made every day a little bit better."

"That sounds pretty good so far," she said.

"Being with you makes me happy," he told her, "and the only way I could imagine being any happier would be with you as my wife. But I don't just want to be your husband, I want to be your partner in every aspect of your life. I want to share your hopes and dreams, to help raise your children, to celebrate with you when you're happy and hold you when you're sad. I want to share every moment of the rest of your life, and that's why I'm asking, Georgia Reed, will you marry me?"

She blew out a shaky breath. "I don't have any words that can top that."

"There's only one word I want to hear," he said.

"Yes." She pressed her lips to his. "Yes, Matthew Garrett, I will marry you."

"You haven't even looked at the ring," he chided.

Because it seemed so important to him, she dropped her gaze to the box in his hand. And this time when her breath caught in her throat it was because she was absolutely stunned by the enormous princess-cut diamond set in a platinum band.

"So it's not about the bling?" he teased, slipping the ring onto her finger.

She couldn't deny that she liked the way the diamond sparkled on her finger, but far more precious to her was the love in his heart. A love that matched her own.

"No," she said, and kissed him again. "It's all about the man."

Georgia had hoped to keep the news of their engagement on the QT for a while—at least until she had a chance to get used to it herself. She didn't count on the fact Charlotte could sniff out a diamond at twenty paces. Georgia had barely walked into the kitchen the next morning when her mother let out a squeal of delight and snatched up her daughter's hand for a closer inspection.

"Look at the size of that rock," she said approvingly. "If that doesn't say 'I love you,' nothin' does." But then her gaze narrowed. "So why is it that your cheeks are glowin' but there's worry in your eyes?"

"I guess I'm just feeling a little like I'm venturing into new territory."

"You were married once before," Charlotte reminded her.

"I know, but everything was different with Phillip. I felt safe with Phillip."

"You're feelin' vulnerable," her mother guessed.

She nodded.

"Every time you put your heart out there, you put it at risk," Charlotte acknowledged. "You just have to trust that it's worth the risk."

"I loved Phillip, but it was a comfortable kind of love. What I feel for Matt is so much more intense, so much more all-encompassing. So much more...everything."

"Love can be scary," her mother agreed. "It's both exhilaratin' and terrifyin', much like those roller coasters you enjoyed so much as a kid."

"That was Indy," Georgia reminded her. "I *hated* roller coasters."

Charlotte chuckled. "That's right. You used to scream

bloody murder whenever your sister convinced you to strap yourself into one."

"She didn't convince me—she bribed me." Usually by offering her share of the cotton candy or caramel corn Charlotte had bought for them. Georgia would happily devour the treat—and then promptly throw it up again when she got off the ride.

And she couldn't help wondering if she was making the same mistake now. The idea of a future with Matt was like a trip to the carnival—both thrilling and terrifying. She had never loved anyone as she loved him, which meant that no one had ever had so much power to break her heart.

But when she was in Matt's arms, she had absolute faith that he wouldn't do so. He was like the safety bar that held her tight, that would keep her in the car, protect her through all of the ups and downs and corners and curves. He would be the partner who shared not just her life but her hopes and her dreams, and a father for her children.

When Phillip died, she'd mourned for her children even more than she'd mourned for herself. She'd cried for her sons who had absolutely doted on their father, and who had been devastated to know that he was never coming home again. And she'd cried for her unborn child who would never even know her daddy. But she hadn't cried for herself, because the truth was, she'd been living life on her own for a long time before she buried her husband.

"So when's the weddin'?" Charlotte asked.

"We just got engaged," Georgia reminded her.

"Which means it's time to start thinkin' about a weddin'," her mother insisted. "Better yet, let's go out today to find you a dress."

"I'm not rushing into anything," Georgia protested.

"But it would mean so much to me to see my baby girl happily married before I go back to Montana."

She shook her head. "There's no way I'm planning a wedding in two weeks."

"You don't need to do a lot of plannin'," Charlotte said, her eyes twinkling. "You and your fiancé can just fly down to Vegas—"

"No."

Her mother frowned. "Why not?"

"Because I don't want to get married by a second-rate Elvis impersonator in some tacky chapel..." She felt the flood of color in her cheeks as her brain finally halted the flow of words from her mouth. "I'm sorry. I didn't mean—"

Charlotte waved off her apology. "Most of those chapels are tacky, but some of those Elvises are real good. Not the one who married me and Trigger, mind you, but I didn't care about the settin' so much as the vows." Then she winked. "And the weddin' night."

Georgia cringed. "Too much information."

"Honestly, Georgia May Reed, I don't know how any daughter of mine grew up to be such a prude."

"Did you know that the word 'prude' provides the root of the word 'prudence,' meaning the exercise of sound judgment?" she asked, undaunted by the criticism.

"Nothin' would show more sound judgment than movin' forward with your life with that sexy doctor," Charlotte told her. "And I'd feel so much better about goin' back to Montana if I knew you were settled and taken care of. But if you won't do it for me, do it for your children."

Georgia narrowed her gaze. "Don't you use my children to manipulate me."

"I'm just askin' you to consider how happy they'd be to have a full-time daddy in their lives again. Especially the twins, since they'll be startin' kindergarten soon." Her mother refilled her mug with coffee, added a heaping teaspoon of sugar. "When they're asked to draw those pictures of their family, I'm sure they'd like bein' able to put a daddy in the scene."

It was, as Charlotte had to know, the only argument that could sway Georgia from her conviction not to rush into anything.

Matt was surprised but not opposed when Georgia suggested a date for their wedding that was less than two weeks away. And he was determined that doing it on short notice didn't mean they couldn't do it right. While Georgia went shopping with her mom for a dress and made arrangements for a minister, flowers and cake, he enlisted the aid of his brothers to get the upstairs bedrooms ready for the kids.

He'd let the twins decide what they wanted for their room and was pleased with the sports-themed border and green paint they selected. Since the room had been empty, he ordered new furniture for them, too—a set of bunk beds, and dressers and desks. Georgia picked out the paint for Pippa's room and lace curtains for her window and pitched in with the decorating whenever she could spare a few minutes in between taking care of the kids and dealing with wedding details.

They were both so busy that they rarely had any time alone. And when they did manage to steal a few minutes of private time, they usually only stayed awake long enough to make love and then fall asleep in one another's arms. But as the date of the wedding drew nearer, Matt knew they needed to find time to talk. Except that now, with the wedding only a few days away, he couldn't help but worry that he'd already waited too long.

He was in the midst of hanging the border in the twins' room when he remembered that he needed a utility knife. When Georgia walked in to check on his progress, it seemed logical to ask her to get the knife out of the top drawer of his desk. It wasn't until she'd started down the stairs that he remembered the photo that was in that same drawer.

Panic clawing at his belly, he dropped the border and raced after her, desperate to get to her before she opened that drawer. But when he reached the doorway, he saw that he was already too late.

Georgia stood behind the desk, the utility knife in one hand and a wallet-sized photograph in the other. He couldn't see the picture from where he was standing, but the image was burned into his mind. A six-year-old boy with dark hair, dark eyes and a broad grin, wearing a mortarboard and gown and holding a rolled-up scroll. Liam's kindergarten graduation photo.

He took a tentative step into the room. "Georgia?"

She looked up at him, and his heart broke to see the doubts and confusion swirling in her eyes. "Who is he?"

He blew out a breath. "His name's Liam.... He was my son."

Chapter Sixteen

Georgia could only stare at him, uncomprehending. She thought he'd said "my son" but that wasn't possible. There was no way he could have a child he'd never mentioned. But the expression on his face—a combination of guilt, regret and remorse—was silent confirmation of his words.

She sank into the chair behind the desk. "You have…a child?"

"I did," he said. "For almost three years."

Three years? But that didn't make any sense either, because the boy in the photo was clearly more than three years old.

"Maybe you could fill in some more details," she suggested, still trying to wrap her head around this sudden and unexpected revelation.

He nodded, but he didn't say anything right away, and she knew that he was struggling to find the right words to explain the situation.

"I married Lindsay because she was pregnant," he finally

said. "And because she told me the baby was mine. It turned out that he wasn't."

Though his words were casual, she heard the tension—and the hurt—in his tone, and her heart ached for him. She could only imagine how he'd responded to the disclosure. And because she knew Matt fairly well now, she knew he wouldn't have just felt hurt and betrayed, he would have been wrecked. "How did you find out?"

"Liam's real father finished his tour of duty in Iraq and decided to track down his ex-girlfriend, only to find that she'd married someone else less than two months after he was deployed."

"Did he know that she was pregnant?"

"No. Apparently Lindsay didn't even know when he left. And even when she knew she was going to have his baby, she didn't want to tell him because she was convinced he would never make it home. Instead, she decided to find another father for her baby."

As a mother, Georgia understood wanting what was best for her children, and she would—without question—do absolutely anything to protect them. But she couldn't imagine any woman being as coldly calculating as Matt was describing this woman to be.

"And I was the perfect patsy. She'd known me for years, because of my friendship with Kelsey. We'd even gone out a couple of times in high school, but it had never gone any further than that. Then suddenly she comes back from California after several years away, spinning this tale about how she never stopped thinking about me. She was beautiful and determined, and I let myself be flattered and seduced."

"She knew you would do the right thing," Georgia guessed. And it made her furious to think that this kind, generous, wonderful man had been ruthlessly targeted for those qualities.

He nodded. "I never even hesitated. I wasn't in love with her but I already loved the baby we were going to have together, and I believed our affection for one another would grow during the course of our marriage."

"I'm so sorry, Matt." And she was, her heart aching for everything he'd gone through.

Having witnessed firsthand how effortlessly he'd connected with her children, it was all too easy to imagine the deep and immediate bond he would have formed with a baby he believed was his own. And when the truth came out, he would have been absolutely devastated.

But he still wouldn't have turned his back on the child. Blood ties or not, in every way that mattered, he had been the little boy's father. His next words confirmed it.

"When Lindsay told me that she wanted a divorce so that she could take Liam back to California to be with his real dad, I was stunned and furious. So much that I thought about suing for custody.

"Although I wasn't Liam's biological parent, Jack assured me that I had a good chance of success, that the courts wouldn't look kindly on Lindsay's blatant deception and might believe that maintaining the status quo was in the child's best interests."

"What changed your mind?" she asked, though she suspected she already knew the answer to that question.

"Seeing the three of them together. It was immediately obvious to me that Lindsay and Jarrod loved one another in a way that she and I never had. And when he first saw Liam, when he realized that he was looking at his son—" Matt cleared his throat. "I just couldn't deny them the chance to be a family."

"Even though it broke your heart," she said softly.

He didn't deny it.

"Do you see him anymore?"

"Not since they moved back to California. Lindsay sends a card and a picture every once in a while, but Liam—" his gaze shifted to focus on the watercolor on the wall behind her "—he doesn't even remember me."

Georgia knew that was likely true. Even the twins' memories of their father were starting to fade. She knew they wouldn't ever forget Phillip—she would make sure of that—but their recollections would dim. For her, that sad truth had been countered, at least in part, by the pleasure of watching her sons bond with Matt.

She looked down at the photo again, her heart aching for the little boy who had been a pawn in his mother's game, thoughtlessly shifted from home to home, from father to father. As a result, Matt had lost his son. And then he'd moved in next door to a woman with three children who had lost their father. But the implications of that were something she wasn't ready to examine too closely just yet.

"This was his kindergarten graduation," she guessed.

He nodded.

She had to moisten her lips before she could ask, "How long ago was that?"

"A few weeks."

So much for thinking that the photo had been in the drawer for so long he'd forgotten about it. He'd only received it a few weeks earlier, and she didn't—couldn't—understand why he'd never mentioned it to her.

"I know I should have told you," Matt began.

And she waited, wondering what explanation he could possibly come up with that might make sense of the whole situation for her. He'd told her about his marriage—no, he'd only told her about his divorce, she realized now. When she'd asked him why he wasn't married, he'd only said that he was divorced. He'd never given her any details and he'd certainly never mentioned that his wife had given birth during the course of their marriage.

Even if it had turned out that the child wasn't his, it was a pretty significant omission. And it made her wonder why he'd been so closemouthed about the situation. In the beginning, okay. She hadn't spilled all the details about her marriage the first time they'd met. But as they'd grown closer, she thought he'd opened up to her. For God's sake, he'd asked her to marry him, their wedding was only three days away, and he'd never given her the tiniest glimpse into this part of his life.

Maybe she should have asked. Certainly his ease with her children, especially with Pippa, should have been a major clue that he had experience with kids. But when she'd questioned why he didn't have half a dozen children of his own, he'd never mentioned that he'd once had a son. He hadn't said anything at all.

Just like he didn't say anything else now, and Georgia finally understood that he wasn't going to. He wasn't going to explain why he hadn't told her about the beautiful little boy who had been his son. She knew it couldn't be easy for him to talk about Liam, to remember the child he'd loved and who had been ripped from his life. She could understand that experience would leave a huge hole in anyone's heart. But this wasn't just anyone, it was Matt—the man who claimed to love her.

And now she couldn't help but wonder if his affection for her was real, or if he just missed being a father.

He'd always been so good with her kids—forging a deep and enduring connection with each of them. At first, it had worried her, how quickly and easily the twins had taken to their neighbor. And Pippa hadn't been far behind. The little girl had never known her father, but she lit up like a neon sign whenever Matt walked into the room.

But Georgia's wariness had slowly faded and she'd been

grateful that she'd fallen in love with a man who so obviously loved her children. *I wasn't in love with her, but I already loved the baby we were going to have together.*

As Matt's words echoed in her mind, she had to wonder what had been the precipitating event in their relationship: his attraction to her or his affection for her children?

"Say something, Georgia, please."

She searched for words—any words—to describe the chaos of emotions churning inside of her. In the end, she only said, "Yes, you should have told me."

And she handed him the utility knife and walked out.

Georgia had introduced Trigger to the twins as Henry, not wanting to explain the origin of his nickname, but as soon as they found out he was married to Gramma, they decided that made him their Grampa. The boys had never had a Grampa before and Trigger had seemed so pleased with the designation that she didn't bother to nix the boys' decision.

And Gramma and Grampa were more than happy to look after the kids while Georgia ran some errands. At least that was the excuse she gave for going out again as soon as she'd returned from next door. And she probably did have errands that she needed to run, but in the moment, she couldn't remember any of them with all the doubts and insecurities churning in her mind.

She needed to talk to someone—she needed to vent and cry and try to figure out what Matt's revelation meant for their future. But she still didn't know very many people in Pinehurst and the one person she might consider talking to—Kelsey—had been Matt's friend for a long time.

She'd known me for years, because of my friendship with Kelsey.

That part of his explanation hadn't really registered at the time. In comparison to all of the other details, it had hardly seemed significant. But now Georgia knew that Kelsey might be the one person who had some of the answers she so desperately needed.

She walked down Main Street, past Emma's Flower Shop and Beckett's Sporting Goods until she found herself in front of Postcards from the World—Travel Agents & Vacation Planners.

Kelsey spotted her as soon as she walked through the door and waved her over. "Matt said you guys weren't going to plan a proper honeymoon until you'd weaned Pippa, but I had some ideas...." Her excited chatter faded away as Georgia got closer. "Obviously you're not here to inquire about vacation destinations."

"No, I'm not," Georgia agreed. "And I probably shouldn't have just dropped in, but I was hoping you might have a few minutes."

Kelsey looked around the mostly empty room. "Right now I have a lot of minutes. Did you want a cup of tea?"

Georgia nodded. "That would be great."

There was a small kitchen in the back, and Kelsey gestured for her to sit while she filled the kettle and put out a plate of cookies. When the tea was ready, she took a seat across from Georgia and said, "What did he do?"

Georgia wasn't surprised that the other woman had so quickly zeroed in on the heart of the problem, and the bluntness of the question encouraged her to respond equally succinctly. "He forgot to mention that he had a son."

"Are you saying that he didn't tell you until today?"

"He didn't tell me at all. I found a graduation photo of a little boy in his desk."

Kelsey winced. "Sometimes I wonder how that man ever got through medical school with only half of a working brain." Then she sighed. "Of course, he's not really an idiot, he just leads with his heart instead of his head sometimes.

That's why it was so easy for Lindsay to manipulate him. She played her cards exactly right to get what she wanted from Matt."

"Sounds like you knew her well," Georgia commented.

Kelsey paused with her cup halfway to her lips. "What did he tell you about my connection to his ex-wife?"

"He just said that he knew her because of his friendship with you. I assumed that meant you were a friend of hers, too."

The other woman shook her head. "Lindsay is my sister."

Now Georgia felt like the idiot. "I should have realized... I know Brittney calls him 'Uncle Matt,' but I thought that was just because you and he were such close friends."

"She refers to Jack and Luke as 'uncle' for that reason," Kelsey acknowledged. "But there's a real family connection to Matt through his marriage to my sister."

Georgia sipped her tea and tried to assimilate all of this new information.

"What are you thinking?" Kelsey asked gently.

"I don't know what to think. My head is spinning with so many questions and doubts that I don't know if I can articulate any of them."

"I can understand the questions, but what are you doubting?"

"Matt's reasons for wanting to marry me."

"The fact that he's head over heels in love with you isn't enough?"

"Is he?" Georgia asked, finally speaking her greatest fear aloud.

Kelsey looked startled by the question. "Do you really doubt it?"

"He married Lindsay to be a father to her baby," she reminded the other woman. "How do I know he isn't marrying me to be a father to my kids?" It was a possibility that tore at Georgia's heart.

"Ask him," Kelsey said. "That's the only way you can be sure."

It was good advice. Georgia certainly agreed that she and Matt needed to do a lot more talking, but first she went home to nurse her baby and hug her boys. Being with her children always helped her put things in perspective, through all of the best and worst times in her life. Since Matt had come into their lives, they'd enjoyed some of the best, and losing him, if that were to happen, would be one of the worst.

A short while later, Charlotte tracked her down in the laundry room where she was folding clothes.

"Did you pick up your wedding dress while you were out?"

Georgia shook her head. "No, I forgot."

"Forgot?" Her mother laughed. "How could you forget when you're gettin' married in three days?"

"I don't know if there's going to be a wedding," she admitted.

"Don't be silly," Charlotte chided. "Of course, there's goin' to be a weddin'. The church is booked, the flowers and cake have been ordered, and I know two very handsome boys who are lookin' forward to walkin' their mama down the aisle."

Georgia's eyes filled with tears. "This is all happening too fast. I knew Phillip three *years* before we got married—I've barely known Matt three *months*." She swallowed around the tightness in her throat. "And as it turns out, I'm not sure I really know him at all."

Charlotte waved a perfectly manicured hand. "You're just havin' some pre-weddin' jitters. Not to worry—every bride does."

"Mom, I'm not a virgin bride fretting about my wedding night," Georgia said, frustration evident in her tone. For once she wished her mother could be her mother, not the cliché-spouting Southern Belle that she played so well.

"Then tell me what it is about."

So, with no small amount of reservation, she did.

Charlotte was silent for several minutes after Georgia had finished talking, and when she finally spoke, it was only to ask, "Do you love him?"

"It's not that simple," she protested.

"Do you love him?" her mother asked again.

"You know I would never have let him put a ring on my finger if I didn't."

Charlotte nodded. "But do you know that marriage is a leap of faith as much as a testament to love?"

"How am I supposed to trust a man who hasn't been honest with me?"

"He should have been more forthcomin'," Charlotte agreed. "But I don't think you can say he was dishonest. I mean, he never actually told you he didn't have a son, did he?"

"That doesn't make it okay."

"I'm not sayin' it's okay." Her mother's tone was placating. "I'm just sayin' that you need to cut him some slack. No one's perfect, baby girl, and if you expect him to be, you're just goin' to be disappointed."

"You're right," Georgia finally said, because it was easier to agree with her mother than to expect that she might ever see things from her daughter's perspective.

"I understand why you might question his motivations," Charlotte said now. "But you might also consider that he's been so focused on his future with you that he wasn't thinkin' about the past. His ex-wife and her little boy are his past, you and your children are his future.

"You can postpone the weddin'—cancel it even, if that's what you feel you have to do," her mother continued. "But before you make that decision, make sure you think about all of the consequences."

"The boys would be so disappointed," Georgia admitted.

Charlotte shook her head. "Though you're right that puttin' off the weddin' would likely break their hearts, this isn't about my grandbabies. It's about you and about why you said yes when he proposed to you in the first place."

"Because I love him," she admitted.

Her mother looked her in the eye. "And are you willin' to spend the rest of your life without the man you love?"

* * *

After her conversation with her mother, Georgia had gone next door to talk to Matt, only to find out—from his brother Jack, who was cursing as he attempted to assemble bunk beds—that he'd been called in to the hospital. So she went back to her mother's house, but she kept peeking out the window to watch for his return.

It was late when she saw his headlights turn in the driveway, but their conversation couldn't wait any longer. Knowing his routine, she slipped on a pair of sandals and went out the back door. Sure enough, Matt was out on the back deck, watching the puppies run around on the grass. The sky was black, but the moon and the stars gave off enough light that she was able to navigate her way across the yard.

The puppies spotted her first and greeted her with a cacophony of ecstatic barks, jumping at her heels as she made her way to where Matt was sitting.

"Hey," he said, trying for casual, but she heard a world of uncertainty in that single syllable.

She sat down beside him. "Hey, yourself."

Finnigan and Frederick were jumping all over one another, vying for her attention, so she took a moment to play with them while she tried to find the right words to say what she wanted to say.

But Matt broke the silence first, cautiously asking, "Are you still mad?"

She considered the spectrum of emotions that had churned through her system over the past twelve hours. "Mad isn't even part of what I was feeling," she told him. "Unless you count being furious with your ex-wife for what she did to you."

"I wish there was something I could say or do to explain," he said, "but I honestly don't know that there's any explanation."

"You're an idiot?" she suggested.

He managed a smile. "You've been talking to Kelsey."

Georgia nodded.

"I am an idiot," he agreed. "Because the absolute last thing I ever wanted to do was to keep anything from you."

"Then can I ask you something?"

"Anything," he promised.

"Why did you ask me to marry you?"

He shifted so that he was facing her. "That's your question?"

She nodded again.

"I screwed up even worse than I thought if you don't know how much I love you."

"I know you said you do," she acknowledged. "But I need to know that you want to be with me and didn't just see the widow next door and her fatherless kids as an opportunity to have a family again."

"Obviously you know how much I care about Quinn and Shane and Pippa, but as completely as your children won my heart, I never would have proposed to you if I didn't want to be with *you*.

"We've both been married before," he reminded her. "And I don't know about your vows, but I'm pretty sure that mine included something like 'so long as we both shall live' and not 'until the kids grow up and go off to college.'"

She had to smile at that. "The difference this time being that the kids aren't an obscure concept but an immediate reality."

"I couldn't love Quinn and Shane and Pippa any more if they were my own, but I wasn't thinking about them when I proposed to you," he assured her. "When I asked you to marry me, I wasn't thinking about teaching Quinn to throw a curveball or watching Shane knock it out of the park or even about the huge princess party we're going to throw for Pippa's first birthday."

"Although you've obviously given all of those ideas some thought."

"Because when I think of the future with you, it encompasses everything that I've ever wanted, but none of it matters without you." He took her hands, linked their fingers together. "I asked you to marry me because when I thought about my future, I couldn't imagine it without you. The kids are a bonus—I won't deny that—but it's you that I want by my side for the rest of my life."

The sincerity in his tone, the depth of emotion she could read in his eyes, brought tears to her own.

"But if you want to reschedule the wedding, that's okay," he told her. "Just don't push me out of your life. Give me a chance to prove how much I love you. Please."

"Do *you* want to reschedule?"

"No," he replied without hesitation. "I want to spend the rest of my life with you, and I want the rest of our life together to start as soon as possible. But if you've got any doubts at all…"

She shook her head, because she didn't. Not anymore. "I don't want to postpone the wedding," she said. "I want to marry you because I love you, and I want the rest of our life together to start as soon as possible."

He hauled her into his arms and kissed her firmly. And then he drew back to say, "In the interest of full disclosure—"

Georgia instinctively tensed. "Is this another secret from your past?"

"No, it's an idea for our future."

She exhaled. "Okay."

"I just wanted you to know that I've thought about someday adding to our family."

"You'd want more children?" She hadn't considered the possibility. Maybe because Pippa was still just a baby, the idea of having another baby had never crossed her mind. But now that Matt had mentioned it, she knew that she would love to have another child—Matt's child.

"Only if you do," he hastened to assure her. "I just thought, we've already got two boys, it might be nice for Pippa to have a sister."

It was the *we* that had her eyes filling with tears, the ease with which he'd spoken that one word that made her accept the truth of his feelings for her. He hadn't put the ring on her finger to make them a family—they already were a family. The ring really was about his love and commitment to her.

"Why don't we hold off any discussion about another baby until I've finished nursing this one," Georgia suggested.

"That sounds fair," he agreed.

"Besides, we have more important things to do right now if we're going to move into your house after the wedding in three days."

"I finished hanging the border in the twins' room," he told her. "Do you want to see it?"

"You're just trying to get me upstairs, conveniently down the hall from your bedroom," she guessed.

He smiled. "Am I that transparent?"

She framed his face in her hands so that she could look into his eyes and clearly see his love for her shining through.

"Yes, you are," she said, and touched her lips to his.

"I love you, Georgia Reed."

"And I love you, Matt Garrett," she told him. "Now, let's go check out that border."

He took her hand and led her into the house that was no longer his own but the home they would share—just like their future—together.

Epilogue

The day of the wedding wasn't very different from any other day that Matt had experienced since moving in next door to Georgia and her kids—which meant that it was pretty much chaos from beginning to end.

He knew it was his own fault, since he'd convinced his bride-to-be to let the twins spend the night at his house. He'd been confident that he could handle the routines of two little boys and get them ready for church the next day. Besides, he had backup in the form of Jack and Luke.

When the boys were fed and washed and dressed—and looking way too darn cute in their little tuxedos, despite the fact that Quinn kept complaining the shoes were too tight—they wanted to play. But all of their toys were next door, so he put cartoons on the TV. That occupied them for all of about thirty minutes, after which he finally agreed they could go outside with the puppies *so long as they didn't get dirty.*

Both Quinn and Shane nodded their understanding of the rule, and Luke went outside with them to ensure they followed it. Unfortunately, no one could have anticipated that Finnigan would find "something stinky and dead" (as Quinn later described it) in the yard and decide it would make a tasty snack, but not so tasty that he didn't later throw it up on Shane's pants.

Luke—the expert on all kinds of puppy puke—brought them back inside for cleanup. It was shortly after that when Jack discovered Quinn's shoes in the toilet of the downstairs bathroom. Apparently Mommy never let him put wet shoes on his feet for fear he'd catch "new-moan-ya," so he'd stuffed them in the toilet to get them wet and unwearable.

When Matt rounded everyone up for a last inspection before they headed off to the church, he decided that the boys' tuxedos didn't look too bad with running shoes. Then he made the mistake of reminding the twins that they were going to walk down the aisle on either side of their mom to give her away. He said the words without thinking, and both Quinn and Shane burst into tears, protesting that they didn't want to give away their mommy, they wanted to keep her forever and ever.

By the time he dried their tears, clarified their role in the ceremony and confirmed that they were *all* going to be together forever and ever, his head was throbbing.

A grinning Luke handed him a glass of water and a couple of Tylenol. Jack followed that up with a tumbler of scotch.

But all the drama was forgotten as soon as he saw Georgia. Wearing a sheath-style dress of cream-colored lace and carrying a bouquet of red roses, she completely took his breath away.

It seemed to take forever for her to reach the front of the church—which might have been because Quinn and Shane were almost literally dragging their feet—but when the minister instructed them to join hands, Georgia's were steady and warm. And in her eyes, he couldn't see any evidence of lingering doubts, just love and joy shining in the beautiful blue depths.

But as a reminder, in case the vows hadn't been enough, he whispered to her, "I love you, Mrs. Garrett."

"I know," she said. "I love you, too."

And when his lips brushed over hers, he heard Quinn clearly announce, "We gived her away, but she's still our mommy."

As soft chuckles sounded from the gallery, Georgia drew back to look at him, silently questioning.

Matt could only shake his head. "Let's just say that the only thing that got me through the last few hours on my own with those boys was the knowledge that, after today, I would always have you by my side."

"Always," she promised.

As Georgia and Matt made their way back down the aisle, they were flanked by Shane and Quinn with Pippa in her mother's arms.

Now, officially, a family.

* * * * *

Don't miss Jack Garrett's story,
the next installment of Brenda Harlen's new miniseries,
THOSE ENGAGING GARRETTS!

Coming soon to Harlequin Special Edition!

COMING NEXT MONTH
from Harlequin® Special Edition®
AVAILABLE JANUARY 22, 2012

#2239 A DATE WITH FORTUNE
The Fortunes of Texas: Southern Invasion
Susan Crosby
Michael Fortune comes to quaint Red Rock to persuade his cousins to come back to the family business in Atlanta. But when he meets Felicity, an adorable candy maker who owns a local chocolate shop, *she* may hold more weight than he's ready for.

#2240 A PERFECTLY IMPERFECT MATCH
Matchmaking Mamas
Marie Ferrarella
Jared Winterset throws his parents a celebratory party for their thirty-fifth wedding anniversary with the help of party planner and secret matchmaker Theresa Manetti. When he sees the sweet violinist Theresa strategically chose to entertain during the celebration, he winds up finding the woman *he* wants to marry.

#2241 THE COWBOY'S PREGNANT BRIDE
St. Valentine, Texas
Crystal Green
Cowboy Jared Colton has a dark past, and when he comes to St. Valentine to uncover some truth, he finds himself wanting to crack a different mystery…a pregnant bride who is running away from her own secrets.

#2242 THE MARRIAGE CAMPAIGN
Summer Sisters
Karen Templeton
Wes Phillips has proven his worthiness to win a seat in Congress, but does he have what it takes to win and heal Blythe Broussard's wounded heart?

#2243 HIS VALENTINE BRIDE
Rx for Love
Cindy Kirk
He loves her best friend. She, though helplessly in love with him, pretends to like *his* friend. Are they too far into a lie when he realizes that she's the one for him after all?

#2244 STILL THE ONE
Michelle Major
Lainey Morgan ran away with a hurtful secret the day of her wedding to Ethan Daniels. Now that she's beckoned to return and take care of her estranged mother, she's regretting her decision to leave Ethan at the altar. If she confronts him about the reason she fled, will he take her back?

SPECIAL EXCERPT FROM
HARLEQUIN® SUPERROMANCE™

Wild for the Sheriff

by Kathleen O'Brien

On sale February 5

Dallas Garwood has always been the good guy, the one who does the right thing...except whenever he crosses paths with Rowena Wright. Now that she's back, things could get interesting for this small-town sheriff! Read on for an exciting excerpt from *Wild for the Sheriff* by Kathleen O'Brien.

Dallas Garwood had always known that sooner or later he'd open a door, turn a corner or look up from his desk and see Rowena Wright standing there.

It wasn't logical. It was simply an unshakable certainty that she wasn't gone for good, that one day she would return.

Not to see him, of course. He didn't kid himself that their brief interlude had been important to her. But she'd be back for Bell River—the ranch that was part of her.

Still, he hadn't thought today would be the day he'd face her across the threshold of her former home.

Or that she would look so gaunt. Her beauty was still there, but buried beneath some kind of haggard exhaustion. Her wild green eyes were circled with shadows, and her white shirt and jeans hung on her.

HSREXP0113

Something twisted in his chest, stealing his words. He'd never expected to feel pity for Rowena Wright.

She still knew how to look sardonic. She took him in, and he saw himself as she did, from the white-lightning scar dividing his right eyebrow to the shiny gold star pinned at his breast.

Three-tenths of a second. That was all it took to make him feel boring and overdressed, as if his uniform were as much a costume as his son Alec's cowboy hat.

"*Sheriff* Dallas Garwood." The crooked smile on her red lips was cryptic. "I should have known. Truly, I should have known."

"I didn't realize you'd come home," he said, wishing he didn't sound so stiff.

"Come *back,*" she corrected him. "After all these years, it might be a bit of a stretch to call Bell River *home.*"

"I see." He didn't really, but so what? He'd been her lover once, but never her friend.

The funny thing was, right now he'd give almost anything to change that and resurrect that long-ago connection.

Will Dallas and Rowena reconnect? Or will she skip town again with everything left unsaid? Find out in *Wild for the Sheriff* by Kathleen O'Brien, available February 2013 from Harlequin® Superromance®.

HSREXP0113